Brush with Death . . .

The room was very cold, and she began to shiver in her light hospital tunic. A strange smell stung her nostrils; an overpowering chemical odor filled the air. The dark was almost as suffocating as the odor.

Gradually she could make out several banks of high metal tables in the gloom. She started to feel her way around the room, touching the cold metal of the tables as she went.

An unexpected puddle of water made her slip, and she reached out to steady herself. Her hand grasped something on a table . . . Something—

Round.

Freezing.

Familiar.

She was clutching the cold, clammy shoulder of a corpse!

Books by R. L. Stine

Available from ARCHWAY Paperbacks

FEAR STREET®
R.L. STINE

The Knife

AN ARCHWAY PAPERBACK
Published by POCKET BOOKS
New York   London   Toronto   Sydney   Tokyo   Singapore

AN ARCHWAY PAPERBACK *Original*

An Archway Paperback published by
POCKET BOOKS, a division of Simon & Schuster Inc.
1230 Avenue of the Americas, New York, NY 10020

ISBN: 0-671-72484-3

First Archway Paperback printing January 1992

10 9 8 7 6 5 4

Cover art by Bill Schmidt

Printed in the U.S.A.

IL 6+

The Knife

prologue

G̲asping in panic, Laurie slipped past the yellow and black signs warning DANGER! KEEP OUT! and pushed open the forbidden door.

She shouldn't be in here. She didn't want to be here. But where else could she hide?

The light was dim, the shadows deep and frightening in the deserted new hospital wing. The workmen had all gone home, and Laurie was alone, stumbling in the gloom through construction debris.

Maybe he didn't see me.

Maybe he won't follow me.

Maybe I'm safe!

Her long honey blond hair, usually so sleek, had escaped from its pins, and was whipped in tangles around her shoulders. Her pretty face, usually so calm, was a mask of terror.

Desperately, she moved deeper inside the new construction. Wires snaked along the floor and dangled from the ceiling. Twisted cables bulged from holes in the wall, reaching out to clutch at her.

There was a sudden flash of light as the door was opened.

Trapped!

Trying not to make a sound, Laurie hugged the wall on the far side of the huge room. A wire snagged her sleeve. She uttered a little gasp as she twisted herself free.

Then she heard the familiar voice: "Laurie? I know you're in here. You can't hide from me."

Tears of terror started in her eyes.

"Come out, Laurie," the voice urged. "I just want to talk to you. Won't you let me explain?"

Inching along the wall, Laurie felt the blood pounding in her throat. She couldn't see him but she could feel his terrible presence.

"I won't hurt you," the voice said softly.

Did he say that to her too—just before he stabbed her?

Laurie's whole body trembled.

Suddenly, in one great burst of motion, he was

upon her. His hands seized her shoulders and pulled her back roughly.

Laurie tried to scream, but he clapped a hand over her mouth. She felt his hot breath on her cheek.

Now her only thought was, *Where is the knife?*

chapter

1

One Week Earlier

"*H*ey, Laurie! Wait up!"

From halfway down the corridor Laurie Masters turned to see a huge cloud of silver balloons drifting toward her. Bobbing along under them was a short, cute, dark-haired girl, clutching the balloon strings as if the helium could lift her to the ceiling. Skye Keely, Laurie's best friend, rushed up, panting.

"Where's the party?" Laurie asked.

"These are for the kid in Room 901," Skye said. "He's got so many toys and flowers in there already, there's no room for *him*. What are *you* doing on the Children's Floor?"

"I just got assigned here this morning," Laurie said. "Some change from the Orthopedic Floor! You wouldn't believe how many ways people find to break their bones!"

Skye rolled her eyes. "Tell me about it," she said dryly.

"Come on," Laurie said. "I have to deliver these X-rays to the Nurses' Station."

The girls fell into step as they walked down the gleaming corridor and Laurie dropped her X-rays off. They were both wearing the drab tan tunics all student volunteers at Shadyside Hospital wore. But on Laurie's willowy figure, it didn't look bad.

"Meet me in the cafeteria for lunch?" Skye asked.

"Sure. Maybe today's the day you'll find that handsome med student you've been dying to meet. Then you can retire for the rest of the summer and concentrate on your social life."

"Get real! In this?" Skye stopped and gave a one-handed tug to her tunic with disgust. "I don't know how *you* manage to look so put together wearing it. It's not fair!" Skye shook her dark curly hair with envy and despair. "Anyhow, I wouldn't quit now. It's not the worst summer job I've ever had. I've stopped hating you for talking me into it."

A nurse in starched white cap and uniform bustled up the hall, carrying a tray of medicines. She glowered at Laurie and Skye as she came up to them. "Okay, girls. Get on with your work. You can't just stand here chatting all day." Then she was off in a swish of skirt and a squeak of rubber-soled shoes.

"Uh-oh!" Skye said. "That's Nurse Wilton, Edith Wilton. Stay out of her way. They say she actually smiled once, but that was probably before you and I were born. Here's 901. See you at lunch."

Skye pushed open the patient's door and shepherded her balloons inside.

Laurie continued down the hall a few steps.

The noise of construction grew louder as she approached the new wing that would soon become part of the hospital. Outside the heavy door that blocked off the new wing and partly muffled the din, Laurie saw the bright warning signs: DANGER! KEEP OUT!

Inside, the brand-new Franklin Fear Wing was being built with ten million dollars that Franklin had recently donated to Shadyside Hospital. A descendant of the Fear family, Franklin shared a family trait with his ancestor Simon Fear—he liked to have things named for him.

The Fear Wing. Not exactly the greatest name for a hospital wing, Laurie thought with a shiver.

She stopped to listen to the workmen hammering, riveting, and sawing inside. In a sudden lull, she heard a very different sound: A child was sobbing nearby.

She looked around. The quiet sound was coming from Room 903, just across the hall. Laurie crossed to the door and listened to the soft, pitiful, weary weeping that sounded as if it had been going on for a long time.

She knocked softly on the door to Room 903 and quietly tiptoed inside.

A small boy was lying in the high white hospital bed. His head was turned away from the door.

"Hello, there," Laurie said.

The child did not turn toward her. He just continued crying, more softly now, his voice hoarse.

Laurie looked around the room. It was bare of flowers, toys, cards. There was nothing to cheer up a sick, frightened child.

"I came to visit you," Laurie said.

The crying stopped with a small gasp, but the little boy kept his face turned away. He stared out the window opposite the door, ignoring her.

Laurie stepped to the end of his bed to read the medical chart hanging there: "Toby Deane . . . three years old . . . pneumonia." His temperature had been normal for several days, so he should be going home soon. Why was he so unhappy?

She approached the far side of the bed.

"Hi, Toby. My name's Laurie. I work here." She looked down at the small, pale face. His sandy hair was tousled on the pillow, and his nose was sprinkled with sandy freckles. "I'm a student volunteer," Laurie continued in a quiet voice. "I run errands—like, I deliver things, and sometimes I visit people who feel sad and lonely away from home. Is that how you feel?"

Toby hiccuped once and sniffled. Laurie pulled

a tissue out of the box on the side table and dabbed at Toby's wet cheeks. He sniffled again and turned away. Laurie took his small hand in hers.

"I don't blame you. I'd cry, too, if I were stuck in here. But you're almost all better. I bet you'll be going home soon."

A tiny sob escaped from the boy, and he squeezed his eyes tightly shut.

"Don't feel like talking? That's okay. I'll just keep you company for a while." Laurie stroked his soft hand, trying to soothe him. "Would you like me to read to you? I could go get a book and read you a really nice story. Would you like that?"

The door opened abruptly, and Nurse Wilton marched in.

"What are you doing in here?" she demanded.

"I—I was just talking to Toby, to cheer him up," Laurie said.

"Don't waste your time," Nurse Wilton said brusquely. "He won't talk to you. He won't talk to anyone. You're only bothering him. And you're in the way here, anyhow. Will you please leave."

Laurie was stung by the nurse's harsh tone. But she reminded herself that most nurses were terribly overworked and could get pretty grouchy. One of her friends at Shadyside High, Mayra Barnes, said that her mother, who was also a nurse, was always tired and cranky.

As Laurie left the room she glanced back once more at Toby. He was watching her now, his tear-filled eyes staring at her from behind Nurse Wilton's broad back.

Laurie felt a sudden jolt. She was sure that, silently, the child was pleading with her.

chapter
2

"What kind of meat is blue?" Skye asked as she plunked her tray down across the table from Laurie.

"Today's stew," Laurie answered. "Why didn't you just get a salad?"

"Too healthy. And I didn't see this up close until I got in the light. Yuck!" Skye settled herself at the table and stared at her plate. Around them, the noise of the cafeteria was deafening. Doctors and technicians in white lab coats bumped and jostled for seats at the long tables. The surgical teams in soft green caps, booties, and coveralls moved in groups searching for places together. Weary relatives of patients sat in hushed isolation as the hectic parade of tray-bearing hospital workers swirled around them.

"Could I borrow a couple of those balloons

you had this morning?" Laurie almost had to shout as she leaned across the table and explained to Skye about Toby Deane. "Maybe they'd cheer him up—if the kid in 901 wouldn't mind."

"He wouldn't even miss them," Skye said. "Just open his door, and the toys fall out. I'll get you a few balloons this afternoon."

A stethoscope dangled above Skye's plate as a nurse leaned over her shoulder to grab a packet of sugar from the center of the table. Skye pushed her stew away and stole a potato chip from Laurie's salad plate. "How many raffle tickets did you buy so far?" Skye asked, crunching the chip and reaching for another.

"Just one," Laurie said, sliding her plate away. "I'm selling them, though, if you want more."

"I've already got the winning one. I'm sure of it! I'm going to buy a brand-new red outfit to match the car as soon as I win!"

Hundreds of Shadyside residents were competing for the red Mercedes-Benz sports car on display in the hospital lobby. It was the prize in a raffle to raise money for the Franklin Fear Wing. Laurie had already sold four books of tickets to neighbors and people in town who found her hard to refuse, even if they had already bought a pocketful.

"Don't trash your old Toyota until they hand you the keys," Laurie warned. "What are you doing this Saturday? You got a date?"

"Two dates. Jim Farrow and Eric Porter."

"Not again!" Laurie said. "No fair." She disapproved of Skye's habit of accepting two dates for the same night, then deciding which one to break.

"I know." Skye shrugged. "I'd trade them both in for Andy Price, whenever you get tired of him."

Laurie sighed. "Like, how about now? I'm seeing him Saturday night. I wish I knew how to break up with him."

Skye slurped her Coke and nodded. "Yeah, I can really see why you'd want to dump him. He's just too good-looking, and too much fun, and his dad is only Dr. Raymond Price, just about the most prominent man in Shadyside."

"Dr. Price is his *step*father," Laurie reminded her.

"Gimme a break!" Skye said. "He's also the administrator of this hospital, so you'd better not rock the boat with Andy while you're working here. What's so wrong with Andy?"

"He's just so aimless, such a goof," Laurie said, jabbing her fork at her salad.

"Not everyone wants to be a doctor like you." Skye really admired Laurie, but sometimes she thought Laurie ought to lighten up a little.

"I don't think Andy's serious about anything," Laurie said, chewing thoughtfully.

"He's serious about you," Skye said.

"That's part of the problem. He's, well,

clutchy. I don't like him trying to tie me down all the time. I have lots of interests, and sometimes I'd like to spend time with other guys."

The white-coated orderly sitting next to Skye gathered up his dirty dishes and left the table. Skye was reaching for another of Laurie's potato chips, when she stopped, hand in midair, and sat up straight in her chair. "Oh, wow! Speaking of other guys, check out who just walked in."

"Who?" Laurie refused to turn and stare.

"Would you believe Tom Cruise!" Skye whispered ecstatically. "It isn't! It couldn't be!"

Laurie had to look. "Right on both counts. It isn't and it couldn't be. Tom Cruise is older, and he doesn't have red hair."

"It's not red."

"Well, reddish. Skye, stop staring at him!" Laurie exclaimed. "He may not be as old as Tom Cruise, but he's too old for you. I bet he's in college. He wouldn't be interested in us."

"He's coming this way!" Skye said breathlessly.

"Is this seat taken?" a deep, pleasant voice asked.

Skye smiled. Up close, the guy was every bit as good-looking as the actor, maybe even cuter. He was tall, with dark blue eyes, and his tight T-shirt showed that he was probably an athlete or someone who worked out with weights. The T-shirt was comical—white with big black letters that said: "Wrong way. Go back." Over one shoulder he had slung the telltale tan tunic that marked him as a fellow student volunteer.

"Be my guest," Skye said, making room. "We were saving it for any student volunteer who wants to join us in taking over the hospital."

"Count me in," he said, laughing as he set down his hamburger and coffee. He was talking to Skye but looking at Laurie. He sat down and leaned across the table to be closer to her. "I'm Rick Spencer, a three-day veteran on the Surgical Floor."

"I'm Laurie Masters, on the Children's Floor this week." She blinked her blue eyes and realized she was suddenly very warm. The source of heat was definitely Rick Spencer and his smile.

"Me too," Skye said. "Ninth floor—Kids and Construction. I'm Skye Keely. Hey, I really like your T-shirt!"

Rick turned to her. "You do? I've got the world's largest collection of T-shirts. It's my only claim to fame." He took a bite of his burger and turned back to Laurie. "How do you like it here?"

"It's great!" Laurie said, responding to Rick's interest. "It's what I've wanted to do all my life, work in a hospital. My aunt warned me I might get bored, but I just love every minute here!"

"Laurie's going to be a doctor," Skye said. "If we ever graduate from Shadyside High."

"No kidding!" Rick said, his eyes fixed on

Laurie as he sipped his coffee. "I'm going into my second year at Southbank College, and I'm thinking about going on to medical school."

"And I'm going to join a high-wire act in the circus," Skye mumbled to herself. Being ignored wasn't her favorite thing.

"I thought I'd better get some hospital experience before I made any heavy plans," Rick said to Laurie. "Why did your aunt think you'd be bored? Is she a doctor here?"

"No," Laurie answered. "A financial consultant. She raised me after my parents died, and she always worries about me."

Above the noise of the crowded cafeteria, a sudden, urgent announcement blared out over the paging system: "Code Blue, Room 903. Code Team to 903, stat." Several doctors jumped up and ran out.

"Uh-oh," Skye said. "Code Blue. They just called a code."

"Huh?" Rick said.

Laurie explained. "That's when a patient goes into cardiac arrest, like the heart stops, or there's some other terrible emergency. There's a special medical team responsible. They can save a life if they get there fast enough. You just saw some of them running out."

"I guess I have a lot to learn. I didn't hear or see anything." Rick's expression suggested that he hadn't heard or seen anything except Laurie.

The announcement repeated: "Code Blue, Room 903, stat!"

"You'll get used to it—" Laurie told him. Her mouth fell open in shock. Room 903 was little Toby Deane's room. The Code Team had been called for him!

She pushed back her chair and ran out of the cafeteria.

chapter
3

"Where's the fire?" Nurse Jenny Girard raised her head from her papers as Laurie dashed past the ninth-floor Nurses' Station. Laurie didn't stop to answer. She flew down the hall, wondering why everything was so calm in such an emergency.

The door to Room 903 was closed, but she could hear Toby's terrified cries inside. She pushed open the door and stopped, stunned. Nurse Wilton was bending over Toby's bed. The child was thrashing and screaming as he tried to kick her away.

Nurse Wilton looked over at Laurie. "You again?" She straightened up, and Laurie could see the hypodermic needle in her hand. "What's your name?" she demanded.

Laurie told her, stuttering slightly.

"I told you before to get out!" The nurse grabbed Toby's arm as he tried to slide away from her.

"I—I heard them call a Code Blue for Room 903," Laurie explained.

"That was Room 503—not the Children's Floor," Nurse Wilton snapped. "I'm trying to draw blood here, and you're just making it harder."

Toby stared at Laurie as he gasped for breath through his tears.

"Maybe I can help. If I talk to him, hold his hand, he may not mind the needle so much," Laurie pleaded with the nurse.

"Just get out—right now," Nurse Wilton growled. "You student volunteers are more trouble than help!"

Defeated, Laurie gave Toby an encouraging smile, then turned and left. As she walked down the hall, she was so distracted that she almost crashed into an orderly wheeling a cart of lunch dishes around a corner.

She headed for the Nurses' Station. Maybe Nurse Jenny Girard could give her a clue about how to help Toby without bringing Nurse Wilton down on her head again.

At the station, Nurse Girard was arguing sympathetically with an agitated woman. "I'm sorry, Mrs. Deane. I know how eager you are to take your son home, but the doctors won't release him until they're sure he's out of danger."

It was Toby's mother, a large woman in a shapeless dress. Her fingers were clutching her pocketbook so tightly that Laurie could see her white knuckles even from a distance. "Try not to be upset," Nurse Girard urged her. "It won't be long now. He's doing fine. Maybe he can even go home tomorrow."

Laurie wanted to talk to Mrs. Deane, but she was afraid of making her more upset. She watched the woman get into the elevator, then turned back to the Nurses' Station. Nurse Wilton was heading down the hall away from her.

Now was her chance! Moving quickly, she slipped back inside Toby Deane's room.

He was quiet now, just staring out the window.

"Hello, Toby. It's Laurie again. I know it's rough, but I just heard some good news about you."

He didn't move.

"Really! The nurse said you would be going home very soon. Isn't that great!"

Toby turned his tear-stained face to Laurie.

"Maybe even tomorrow."

A flicker of hope lit the small face on the pillow.

"Your mommy will come and get you."

Toby turned away without speaking and closed his eyes. Laurie went to the side of the bed and held his soft hand. His breathing became regular. Just before he fell asleep, Laurie felt his small fingers squeeze hers.

She tiptoed out.

Across the hall, the ominous signs in front of the new Fear Wing assaulted her eyes: DANGER! KEEP OUT! She shuddered. Why did they frighten her so?

As she watched, she saw the door to the Fear Wing close—very slowly. Why would anyone be inside at this time of the day? All the workmen left during lunchtime. She had the distinct feeling that someone was hiding there, maybe watching Toby's room—or watching *her*.

She started down the hall, the hairs on the back of her neck rising. She couldn't help but glance back at the door to the new wing. She caught sight of a man starting out the door. He quickly ducked back inside when he saw her.

It was only a flash, but Laurie thought she caught a glimpse of a tan tunic, of a black-and-white T-shirt.

It was Rick Spencer, the new student volunteer she and Skye had met in the cafeteria.

chapter
4

*T*he street outside was dark. Curled up on the sofa, Laurie turned a page in the book she was reading and checked her watch again. After ten. Her aunt Hillary certainly was working late.

Laurie snuggled down deeper into the sofa in their large, comfortable library, wishing that Hillary would get home soon. Their big old house in North Hills could get very lonely sometimes.

Still, she was very proud of her aunt. Hillary Benedict was one of the most successful financial auditors for miles around. Her work as a consultant to banks and large institutions often took her out of town for days, or kept her out late at night.

Laurie gazed out the window at the dark night and let her thoughts wander. She couldn't remember ever living anywhere except with her aunt. Her parents had been killed in a boating accident when she was very little, and Hillary, her mother's sister, was the only family she could remember. They looked so much alike that most people mistook them for mother and daughter.

In many ways Laurie thought she was lucky. Her friends were always complaining about how their parents tried to control their lives. Hillary gave Laurie lots of space, except when she was worried. But now it was Laurie's turn to worry.

She checked her watch again. Ten-thirty. Where *was* she?

The phone rang. Laurie answered it, expecting it to be Hillary.

No one spoke. "Hello? Hello?" Laurie repeated.

No reply.

She could hear breathing, like someone listening. Some creeps from school playing phone tricks probably. Didn't they know how *lame* that was?

She was about to slam down the receiver when she heard the faint sound of an ambulance siren coming through it, growing louder. It was a sound she heard every day at the hospital.

The line went dead. Laurie stared at the phone, feeling uncomfortable.

A few minutes later the phone rang again, and she jumped. Reluctantly, she picked it up and said, "Hello?"

"Is this Laurie Masters?"

"Who's this?"

"Rick Spencer. We met in the cafeteria today. You ran out so suddenly that I wondered what was wrong."

"How did you get my number?" Laurie asked.

"Oh—your friend gave it to me."

"Skye?" Why hadn't Skye told her?

"That's right," Rick said. "How come you left so fast? Was there any trouble?"

Laurie began to relax. "No, it was just a mistake. There's a kid on the ninth floor I've been worried about, in Room 903. He's so cute! Three years old and freckle faced, but he cries all the time. I thought they had called the code for him, but it was Room 503." Then she remembered. "Uh, Rick, were you on the ninth floor this afternoon, in the Fear Wing?"

"No. Why do you ask?"

"No reason," she said. "Did you just call me a few minutes ago?"

"Yes, but your line was busy. I wanted to ask you if you were free Saturday night. Maybe we could get together? You know, stranger in town, and all that."

"Oh, I'm sorry, I've got a date." For a minute she really *was* sorry. Then she thought of the person she had seen ducking back inside the hospital wing. Had she been wrong?

"Some other time?" Rick asked.

"Sure," she agreed. "We'll see each other at the hospital. Listen, I've got to go. My aunt may be trying to call, and I want to keep the line free."

"Right. I'll look for you tomorrow," Rick said.

Just as Laurie was hanging up, she again heard the wailing of an ambulance siren through the phone, growing louder in her ear until the connection was cut. It sounded as if Rick was still at the hospital, long after student volunteers had left for the day.

She sat there, puzzled. Then she punched Skye's number on the automatic dial button of the phone, even though she knew that her friend usually went to bed early.

"I know it's late," Laurie said, "but I just wanted to ask you one question. Did you give Rick my phone number?"

"Who?" Skye mumbled. She sounded half asleep.

"Rick, Rick Spencer. The guy we met in the— you know, Tom Cruise."

"Oh, yeah. I mean, no. I didn't give him your number. You want me to?"

"Never mind," Laurie said. "I'll see you tomorrow."

After she hung up, Laurie tried to sort out her confusion. Something wasn't right, but she didn't understand *what*. Had Rick been on her line *twice* that night? Was he the silent caller? What had he been doing at the hospital so late? And wasn't that Rick she had seen at the door of the Fear Wing?

Laurie didn't understand much, but she knew one thing for sure—Rick Spencer was a liar!

chapter

5

Laurie had gone to bed before Aunt Hillary got home. And even though she was up early the next morning, her aunt had already left. Hillary must be working on a really big job, Laurie figured.

She spooned up some cottage cheese for her breakfast as she read the note her aunt had left.

Hi, cookie. Busy, busy. Sorry I missed you last night. Don't look for me for dinner tonight. Working late again. Love you.

H.

Laurie had a special mission that morning, and she was eager to get to the hospital early. She stuffed her tan tunic into her bag, grabbed her car keys, and was annoyed when the phone rang and stopped her before she got out the door.

"This is Dr. Price," the voice said.

"Huh?" Laurie cried in surprise.

"I have a special assignment for you today. I want you to skip work and play tennis with my son."

"Andy!" Laurie laughed. "You're under arrest for practicing medicine without a license. No tennis! No way!"

"Then how about a quick swim?" Andy insisted, switching to his real voice.

"No way. I mean it," Laurie said firmly. "Today is a workday, and I'm in a rush."

"I hardly get to see you this summer," Andy complained. "You're always busy."

"It's your own fault. You could have joined Skye and me at the hospital. Your father would have liked that. There are *guys* who are student volunteers, you know."

"Oh? Like who?"

Laurie sighed. Sooner or later she'd have to deal with Andy's jealousy. "Gotta go. I'll see you Saturday."

"*Wait!* How about meeting me for pizza after work? Jim Farrow and I are going to Patsy's Pizzeria—Skye, too, probably."

Why not? It was better than fixing dinner for herself alone. *Anything* was better than that.

"Okay, I'll see you there. Bye."

As she drove to Shadyside Hospital, Laurie

thought about Toby Deane. She'd do anything to bring a smile to that sad little face. That was her special mission for the morning.

At the hospital she dodged the early-morning traffic on the main floor and hurried to the gift shop. Books and newspapers, toiletries, flowers, candy, fruit baskets, cards, and T-shirts crowded the small space. Also there was a shelf filled with toys and stuffed animals, just right to cheer up a sick child.

Laurie studied the display for a while, then chose a fluffy little teddy bear for Toby. Eager to bring it to him, she was impatient in the line to pay. She joined the mob in the elevator on the ride up to the Children's Floor.

The hall was empty, even the Nurses' Station was unattended. That early in the morning, the nurses were all busy in patients' rooms. As she walked down the ninth-floor corridor, Laurie smiled, anticipating Toby's happy response to her gift.

"Look who came to see you!" she called, holding out the teddy bear as she entered Room 903.

She stopped—stunned.

The room was empty. The bed had been stripped. All the equipment that had crowded the tables and chest top was gone. There was no sign of Toby!

"Oh, no!" Laurie cried. *"He's dead!"*

chapter
6

"Dead!" Laurie repeated, her lips trembling.

Still holding the teddy bear, she dropped the bag and her tunic on the empty bed and ran out to find the floor nurse—someone, *anyone!*

She knew that Toby couldn't have left the hospital so early. Patients weren't discharged until after the staff doctors saw them on their eleven o'clock rounds. What could have happened to him in the night to cause such a tragedy?

At the Nurses' Station she almost skidded to a stop.

There he was, dressed in Oshkosh overalls and a yellow shirt, his hand firmly held by his mother. Laurie was almost weak with relief. Toby Deane was *alive!* He was so cute with his sandy hair neatly combed and the toes of his little sneakered feet turned in toward each other that Laurie could have rushed up and hugged him.

How come they were letting him leave so early?

It was then that Laurie noticed Mrs. Deane was deep in conversation with Rick Spencer. What was *he* doing on the Children's Floor? He had said that he was working on Surgical. And what were he and Toby's mother talking about?

He leaned toward Mrs. Deane as he spoke, holding his tan tunic over one shoulder. That day's T-shirt was black with bright red flames and a big Harley Davidson logo. He certainly has tacky taste, Laurie thought.

As she stood watching them, Toby noticed her at the end of the hall. Laurie smiled and held out the teddy bear. His sad eyes brightened, and he pointed to himself, silently asking, "For me?"

Laurie nodded.

Toby glanced up at the empty Nurses' Station, then at his mother and Rick. They were too engrossed in their conversation to notice him. He slipped out of Mrs. Deane's grasp and walked shyly toward Laurie.

"Teddy would have cried if you had left without him," Laurie said. She put the fluffy stuffed animal in Toby's arms.

He hugged it tightly and buried his face in its soft fur.

"You and he are going to be great friends, right?" Laurie said.

Toby nodded but didn't speak.

"I'm really glad you're going home, but I'll miss you. Promise me that every time you hug Teddy you'll think of me, because I'll be thinking of you."

Toby reached up and took Laurie's hand. He seemed reluctant to leave her.

"You'll feel much better once you get home. Now, won't you say goodbye to me? Just one little word?" Laurie asked.

Toby shook his head.

Resigned, Laurie knelt and hugged him. "Okay, Toby. Be a good boy and be nice to Teddy." She kissed his cheek and turned him toward his mother. "Better go now. Your mommy is waiting for you."

Toby turned back to her.

"She's not my mommy," he whispered, and tears welled up in his eyes.

chapter

7

*L*aurie leaned closer to Toby. "What do you mean? Of course she's your mommy."

Toby shook his head. "No, she's not!"

"Toby! Come here this minute!" Mrs. Deane called. But Rick said something to her just then and distracted her.

"Who is she then?" Laurie asked. She wondered if Toby was still sick and imagining things.

"I'm not supposed to say. She'll be mad if I do."

"Who'll be mad? Who *is* she?"

Toby hung his head. "I want to go home!" He snuffled.

"Toby, I said come *here,* right now!" Mrs. Deane called sharply. Both she and Rick were staring at Laurie and the child.

Dragging his feet, Toby returned to the Nurses'

Station. Laurie could see Mrs. Deane questioning him about the teddy bear, which Toby clutched even tighter. Rick and the woman glanced down the hall at Laurie. Then Mrs. Deane took Toby's hand and pulled him toward the elevators.

Just before he stepped inside, Toby gave Laurie one last pleading look.

Laurie hurried to the Nurses' Station to talk to Rick. He had pulled on his tan tunic and was smoothing his hair when she reached him.

"What are you doing on this floor?" Laurie asked.

"One of the doctors sent me on an errand. Hey, that was really nice of you to get that kid a toy. Toby Deane—is he the one you were worrying about yesterday?"

"Uh-huh," Laurie said. "That woman you were talking to, she's his mother, right?"

"Right," Rick said. "They're new in Shadyside. Just moved into an old house on Fear Street, she told me. I was telling her where the nearest pharmacy is so she can fill a prescription for Toby. I'm glad I ran into you."

"Me too," Laurie said, planning her next words to sound casual. "I was wondering why you were at the hospital so late last night. Have they started night shifts for the volunteers?"

Rick seemed surprised. "What makes you think I was here?"

"Weren't you?"

"Nope." He hesitated. "I was hoping I'd see you here because I wanted to ask you if you're free after work today. I thought maybe you'd like to show a stranger around town."

His dark blue eyes fixed on hers. He smiled, and Laurie had to remind herself that she couldn't trust him any farther than she could throw him.

He *was* at the hospital the night before—she was sure of it. And how could he have directed Mrs. Deane to a pharmacy? He was new in Shadyside himself, he said.

He certainly was laying on the charm, though. And he certainly was sure of himself. "Is it a date?" he asked, touching her sleeve.

"I can't. I'm meeting someone—"

The phone at the Nurses' Station rang, saving her from having to explain any further. No nurse was in sight. Laurie leaned over the high ledge of the station to the desk below it where the phone kept up its jangling. She reached to answer it—but pulled back her hand in alarm.

On the desk next to the phone was a long, rectangular box, its lid open, displaying its frightening contents: Three long surgical knives lay in the fitted case, the light sparkling on their razor-sharp blades.

Laurie stared at them, almost hypnotized.

The phone continued to ring.

"I'll get it," Rick said, reaching around her.

She backed away and let him answer the call.

She couldn't understand why she had been so overcome with terror. Those knives were instruments of healing, designed to help the sick, not to cause pain or injury. Why had they filled her with horror?

I'm too jumpy, she thought as she made her way back to Toby's room to pick up her bag and tunic. The little boy's words haunted her. Why did he say Mrs. Deane wasn't his mother? Was there something seriously wrong with Toby?

When she returned to the hall, she watched as Rick finished writing a note and hung up the phone.

Then she saw him pick up the box of surgical knives, close it, and slip it into the pocket of his tunic as he walked to the elevators.

chapter
8

*R*ick stole those knives!

Laurie couldn't believe her eyes. She stared at the elevator door that had just closed behind him, wondering what to do. She ought to tell someone—but *whom?* And did she really want to get Rick into serious trouble?

He's a thief, as well as a liar, a small voice in her head reminded her.

She went to the Nurses' Station and stood there, scowling in confusion.

A loud clatter from the service elevator around the corner startled her. A troop of workmen erupted into the hallway. They were so noisy and distracting as they marched down to the Fear Wing that Laurie didn't even notice Nurse Jenny Girard return to her desk. When the phone rang, and Laurie turned to answer it, she was surprised to see Nurse Girard pick up the receiver.

Nurse Girard! Laurie thought. Maybe I should mention the knives to *her*.

The tall, dark-haired nurse was laughing into the phone. "What? *More?* I don't believe it! . . . Okay, I'll send someone to pick it up. There's a volunteer standing here right now." She hung up, shaking her head in amusement.

Laurie started to tell her about the knives. "Uh, I wonder—did you see those—?" But the nurse interrupted her.

"Laurie, would you be a doll, please? There's a package down at Reception for Room 901— *another* one! They're going to need a truck to take that kid and his toys home! Would you go pick it up?"

That was the first of dozens of errands that kept Laurie running all day. Everywhere she went, though, she couldn't stop thinking about Toby, about what he had said, Rick all but forgotten now. Toby's small, sad, frightened face floated in front of her as she delivered packages and X-rays, read to patients, and helped the nurses. She was haunted by him.

By the end of the day, Laurie had made up her mind. Toby Deane was in trouble. He needed her help. She *had* to do something.

Patients' records were stored in a small office at the back of the Nurses' Station. No one was allowed in there except doctors and nurses.

Laurie would be taking a terrible chance, but she was determined to see Toby again, and she'd have to check his records to find his address.

After work, when the nurses' shifts were changing and when the workmen from the Fear Wing were all leaving for the day, Laurie took advantage of the confusion to sneak into the office.

Inside, it was cramped and dusty and smelled of old paper. She felt claustrophobic in the tiny space. Her fingers trembling, she flipped through the records until she found Toby's. He did live on Fear Street, as Rick had said. Fear Street was the last place on earth Laurie would want to go. The very name filled her with dread. But if she didn't go to Toby's house, she'd never see him again.

As she made a note of Toby's address, she realized that she needed some kind of excuse to visit him. She couldn't just ring the doorbell and say she had come to see Toby. Mrs. Deane hadn't looked at all friendly. Laurie needed a reason, something convincing. But *what?* She racked her brain for an answer. Then it struck her.

The raffle! She was selling tickets for the hospital raffle for the Mercedes-Benz. Mrs. Deane must have seen the car on her way in and out of the hospital. Laurie could go to Toby's house on the pretext of selling Mrs. Deane a ticket. It would be so simple. *Except—*

Except, did Laurie really want to go to Fear Street alone?

She glanced at her watch and remembered that

she was supposed to meet Andy at Patsy's Pizzeria. Andy and Skye and Jim Farrow. Why not ask them to go with her to Fear Street? It shouldn't be too hard to convince one of them at least.

Satisfied that she had just solved several problems at once, Laurie returned Toby's records to the files and cracked open the door of the cramped office.

A voice floated in from the Nurses' Station through the opening.

"Oh, Edith, I've been looking for you." Cora Marshall, the head nurse on the Children's Floor, was standing with her back to the office door, calling to someone out of sight. "New orders for the patient in 908. Would you come here, please?"

Nurse Edith Wilton stepped up to the front desk.

Laurie inched the door almost shut again and stood in the dark, trembling. Of all the people to catch her, Nurse Wilton would be the absolute worst!

Laurie peeped out and watched the two nurses confer. She was almost frantic as she waited for her chance to escape. It seemed an eternity before Nurse Marshall left. Any minute now Wilton will leave too, Laurie thought. But Nurse Wilton settled in the desk chair and began to go over some charts.

Laurie fidgeted desperately. The small office became even tinier. And warmer. She clenched her fists to calm herself. She thought she would explode.

Nurse Wilton turned a page in the charts, and a sheet of paper fell to the floor. She bent to pick it up. Her head was now below the desk.

Without thinking Laurie darted out of the office, past the desk, and down the hall.

But not fast enough.

"Just a minute, young lady!" Nurse Wilton called. "What were you doing in there?"

Laurie kept going.

"I saw you, Laurie!" the nurse shouted. "Come back here!"

Laurie swerved to avoid a young patient in a bathrobe who was strolling in the hall. She skidded around the first corner. She was out of sight, but she could still hear Nurse Wilton's squishy shoes squeaking down the hall after her.

Dead end!

Laurie came to a full stop at the door to the service elevator. It was only used to transport heavy equipment and patients on gurneys. No other traffic was allowed. But there was no other place for Laurie to go, except straight into Nurse Wilton's arms. She jabbed at the elevator button, whispering, "Hurry! Please!"

The door slid open, and Laurie stepped inside, just as Nurse Wilton rounded the corner.

"Wait!" the furious nurse called.

The door slid shut, and the elevator began to

move slowly downward. Laurie sighed with relief, took a step back—and bumped into a gurney. She wheeled around and looked down in horror.

Lying on the rolling table was a waxen-faced woman, her eyes closed. Monitoring machines whirred and beeped nervously at her feet. Intravenous bottles hung from poles over the gurney, with tubes leading into the woman's body somewhere beneath the blanket. The bottles had started jiggling and clicking when Laurie hit the table.

"Watch it!" the orderly escorting the patient growled. "You're not supposed to be here." His hand gripped Laurie's shoulder and she gasped. He pushed a button on the elevator panel and ordered her, "Out! You're getting off at the next floor."

With pleasure, Laurie thought. She glanced down at the patient on the gurney. *She must be dead!* Suddenly the woman's eyes snapped open. She fixed Laurie with a terrible stare and moaned softly.

Laurie pressed herself against the elevator wall. When the elevator crawled to a stop, Laurie flung herself out through the open door. She didn't know where she was, and she didn't care. Then she saw the sign opposite the elevator door:

THIS FLOOR RESTRICTED
AUTHORIZED PERSONNEL ONLY

The elevator doors closed, and Laurie was alone. She looked around. The hall was quite dark. The whole floor was quiet and seemed to be deserted.

Laurie had never been on this floor before. It didn't look like an ordinary medical ward. Where *was* she? And how was she going to get out?

She was confused and a little afraid to move away from the service elevator. She might get lost in the unfamiliar corridor.

The rumbling and clanking of the elevator's gears startled her, and she looked up at the floor indicator. It had stopped at the ninth floor. The elevator must have dropped off its patient and returned to the Children's Floor.

Nurse Wilton! Laurie thought. She would have seen the indicator stop when Laurie got off. She knew where Laurie was.

She'd be coming to get her!

Laurie had no choice. She had to get away. She started down the dark hall, desperately trying each door as she passed. They were all locked. She didn't know if she was heading for the passenger elevators or away from them. She could end up at another dead end, trapped!

Suddenly, as she went around a corner, she spied something crouched at the end of the corridor.

Something small.

It wasn't moving.

She squinted hard into the shadows. And almost laughed.

It was a cleaning bucket and a mop outside the last door.

If an orderly was in there, he could tell her how to get out. He might scream at her for being on a restricted floor, but she didn't care—just as long as he helped her get away from Nurse Wilton!

She rushed down the hall to the bucket, expecting to see a rectangle of light shining around the last door. But it, too, was dark. The orderly must have taken a break. He'd be back, Laurie reasoned. But she couldn't stand out in the corridor waiting for Nurse Wilton to catch her.

She tried the doorknob.

The door was open.

Laurie ducked inside and stopped to catch her breath.

The room was very cold, and she began to shiver in her light hospital tunic. A strange smell stung her nostrils; an overpowering chemical odor filled the air. The dark was almost as suffocating as the odor.

Gradually she could make out several banks of high metal tables. She started to feel her way around the room, touching the cold metal of the tables as she went.

An unexpected puddle of water made her slip, and she reached out to steady herself against falling. Her hand grasped something on a table . . . Something—

Round.
Freezing.
Familiar.
She was clutching the cold, clammy shoulder of a corpse!

chapter
9

*L*aurie's hand flew up as she recoiled in panic.

A corpse on the table!

And she had *touched* it!

She backed away and started to gag. Then, in a flash, she knew where she was.

That acrid chemical smell in the air must be formaldehyde, used to preserve and disinfect dead bodies! The floor she had stumbled onto was dark and empty because it was part of the medical school, and classes were over for the day. This room must be the anatomy lab, where students dissected and studied the human body.

The *dead* human body.

As her eyes adjusted to the dark, Laurie began

to see the grisly forms of partially dissected corpses and body parts on the tables. She wheeled around and started toward the door, panting in horror.

Just then she heard footsteps outside, followed by the jangling of keys. Then came the sounds of a key turning in the lock and a bucket clanking as it was taken away from the door and down the corridor.

She was locked in!

An animal-like howl escaped from deep in her throat. She flung herself toward the locked door, only to crash into something white and gleaming that clattered as she touched it.

A dangling white skeleton danced before her, one bony arm wrapping itself around her neck!

She leapt backward, reaching out to keep her balance, and found that she had grabbed an icy hand—a hand that ended at the wrist.

Whirling around, she came face to face with a severed head propped up on a shelf. Its eyes were closed, its mouth was gaping, and its scalp had been partially peeled back.

Laurie tried to cry out, but her terror choked in her throat.

She flew to the door, rattling the doorknob, slamming her fists against the solid wood. She didn't care if Nurse Wilton found her. She had to get out of this ghastly room, away from the bodies, the parts of bodies—

She pounded frantically, but nobody was there to hear.

She leaned her forehead against the door for a minute.

Then she had a sickening new feeling. *Something in the room behind her was moving!*

chapter

10

Laurie spun around to face the terrible *thing* that was coming at her. She scanned the dark room, tears filling her eyes. Her breathing was loud in her ears.

Where was it?

What was it?

The room was perfectly still. Nothing was moving toward her. The dark shapes of the tables, each with its grisly burden, lurked silently, unmoving.

She realized that she had become hysterical with terror. She was imagining things. Nothing in the room was alive and stirring, except for *her*.

With that moment of clarity, she realized something else—the door may have needed a key to lock from the outside, but she should be able to unlock it from the inside.

She turned back to the door. Her hand trembling, she felt for the doorknob and twisted it.

The lock held fast.

Her fingers swept around the doorknob, probing for the latch bolt. There it was, a knob of metal protruding from the door just above the knob! She tried turning it to the left.

Nothing.

To the right.

Ah! There was a metallic *clunk,* and the catch released.

In her haste to escape, Laurie nearly stumbled over her own feet. She didn't bother closing the lab door behind her. She just flew down the hall, gulping in deep breaths of untainted air as she ran.

Rounding the curve of the long corridor, she braked to a sudden stop.

Nurse Wilton was standing at the service elevator, her back to the hall. She wasn't alone.

The tall man with her had gray hair and was wearing a white lab coat. He wasn't a security guard, Laurie knew, because they wore blue uniforms.

From the back, he seemed familiar to Laurie. How strange, she thought. Had Nurse Wilton called a *doctor* to help her chase Laurie?

She backed up against the wall and inched around the curve, praying that they hadn't seen her. Their conversation floated down the hall, but Laurie couldn't hear what they were saying—only that Nurse Wilton sounded very upset.

Just as the elevator doors opened, Laurie thought she knew who the man was. He looked very much like Andy's father, Dr. Raymond Price!

Impossible. Nurse Wilton wouldn't call the *head* of Shadyside Hospital to complain about a student volunteer—not unless she was crazy! Laurie knew she must be mistaken.

Right now she had other things to worry about. Like, how to get *out.* As soon as the elevator door closed on the man and Nurse Wilton, Laurie took off to find the passenger elevators.

Once she was out of the hospital and behind the wheel of her car in the parking lot, it took a long time before she could stop shaking enough to drive to Patsy's Pizzeria.

"You got locked in where?" Skye asked as she picked a piece of pepperoni off her pizza and popped it into her mouth. She stared in amazement at Laurie, then at Andy, who were both seated across the table from her.

Patsy's Pizzeria was jammed, as usual. Since it was near Shadyside Hospital, most of the people who went there were on the hospital staff and knew one another. Talking between the tables raised the decibels almost to the level of the hospital cafeteria.

"Listen to this," Skye said to Jim Farrow as he set his oily paper plate of pizza down on the table and sat next to her. "Laurie was locked inside the anatomy lab!"

"It was a nightmare!" Laurie said, shuddering. "Pieces of bodies, and heads, and skeletons—"

"All dripping with slime, I'll bet," Andy said. He picked up his cheesy slice and let the yellow and red ooze onto his plate. "Just like this."

"Come on, man—I'm trying to eat," Jim groaned. He shook his blond head and took a bite of his slice.

"I'd rather touch a corpse than eat those anchovies," Skye said, and turned back to Laurie. "How did you get out? And what were you doing in the anatomy lab anyhow?"

Laurie was suddenly reluctant to tell them that she had been chased there by a nurse who had caught her where she wasn't supposed to be.

"Uh, I got off the elevator on the wrong floor." She shrugged it off, eager to change the subject. "Listen, are any of you free later? I've got an errand to run, and I could use some company."

Between bites of pizza, she told them about Toby Deane—not everything, just that he seemed sad and lonely and she wanted to visit him.

She pulled the booklets of raffle tickets out of her bag and explained that she was going to use them as an excuse to drop by Toby's house. "I was going to go there right away—um, if any of you wanted to come along?"

"Ooh, that *does* sound like a thrill!" Andy exclaimed sarcastically. "It might be too exciting for me."

Laurie tried to hide her embarrassment. "Well, the house is on Fear Street. And I—"

Jim laughed. "And you want someone to hold your hand?"

"Don't laugh at her, Farrow," Skye said scornfully. "You were the one who told everyone that story about being chased by something the size of a bear through the Fear Street woods?"

"It wouldn't stop me from going again, though," Jim protested.

"Okay, we'll *all* go," Skye decided.

"Great," Andy said sarcastically. He wiped his hands carefully, then ran them through his thick dark hair. He looked glum. "Can't we think of anything better to do?"

"If you don't want to come—" Laurie snapped.

"Okay. Okay. I'll go," Andy said moodily.

Thoughts of Fear Street in the dark of night sobered them as they made their way out of the pizzeria a little later and piled into Andy's Volvo. So many frightening stories had been told about this street that wound past the cemetery and through the thick Fear Street woods. Stories that most often turned out to be true. . . .

By the time the four friends turned onto Fear Street, they were all quiet and deadly serious.

"Do you have the address?" Jim asked Laurie, leaning over from the backseat of the car.

Laurie was staring out the window. In the early-evening light, Fear Street didn't look particularly terrifying. But there was a stillness that was unnatural. A heavy silence surrounded them as they drove slowly along the curving road.

Laurie was so transfixed that she jumped when Jim touched her shoulder.

"The address?" he repeated.

"Oh, yes." Laurie pulled the note out of her bag and read the street number out loud.

"That would be a little farther along," Andy said. "Near the cemetery, I think." He slowed the car as they drove closer to the Deanes' number.

"Right here," Skye said. "This should be the house."

They stopped in front of a large gray Victorian mansion, with gingerbread cutouts around its roofline, set back on a deep lawn. But when they got out of the car, they found no number or name to identify the owner of the house.

"I'll check the house next door," Jim volunteered. He jogged over to inspect a similar Victorian. When he returned, he reported that that house, too, had no number and no identifying name on its mailbox.

"It's got to be one of these," Skye said.

"Let's split the raffle tickets," Andy suggested.

"Good thinking," Skye said. "Laurie and I will try this house, and you and Jim go next door."

They separated at the curb. Andy tucked his tickets into the pocket of his cutoffs, and he and Jim started toward the driveway of their house.

Laurie smoothed out invisible wrinkles in her pale yellow slacks as she and Skye walked up the long drive to the house in front of them. She straightened the collar of her soft yellow- and blue-striped blouse. She fiddled with the gold chain belt at her waist and cleared her throat.

"What are you so nervous about?" Skye asked, her voice quieter than usual. She was staring up at the old mansion that loomed before them.

They mounted the steps to the front porch, and Laurie rang the doorbell. They waited, both of them fidgeting, but the door remained closed.

"No one's home," Skye whispered. "Let's go."

"Why are you whispering?" Laurie asked.

"I'm not," Skye whispered again. "Oh, come on! I'm leaving."

Laurie cocked her head. "Wait a minute. Did you hear that?" She stepped back and looked up at the upper floors. "There it is again. That sound—like a cat or something. It came from inside."

"I didn't hear anything," Skye said. The heavy stillness of Fear Street was getting to her, though, and she tugged at Laurie's arm. "Let's get out of here."

55

Just then the door opened. Laurie recognized the woman standing inside, holding the door slightly ajar. It was Mrs. Deane, the woman who had picked Toby up at the hospital. They had found the right house.

Toby's mother stared out at them, a scowl on her face. She was wearing a baggy sweater over an equally baggy dress that was stained down the front. Wisps of frizzy bleached blond hair straggled around her ears, and her pale eyes squinted suspiciously at the girls. She didn't seem to recognize Laurie from the hospital.

"Yes?" she said darkly.

"Hello," Skye began, her voice croaking.

"I'm very busy. What do you want?" Mrs. Deane said.

Laurie stepped closer to the door. "We're student volunteers at Shadyside Hospital," she said, holding up the tickets in her hand. "We're selling raffle tickets for the construction fund there. You know, for the red Mercedes? They cost a dollar each, and we wondered if you'd like to—" She ran the words together nervously.

"Oh, for heaven's sake!" Mrs. Deane said, annoyed. She glanced back over her shoulder into the house.

Laurie tried to peek inside, but Mrs. Deane was blocking her view. So Laurie continued her appeal. "They're holding the drawing in September. It's a fabulous car, and a really good cause. Everyone in Shadyside is—"

"Okay, okay." Mrs. Deane turned back to her. "How much?"

"A dollar a ticket. I've got a full book if you want more."

"One will do," Mrs. Deane said. "I'll have to get my purse." She moved away from the door, and Laurie started to follow her inside. "No! Wait here." She closed the door quickly in Laurie's face.

"Was *that* Toby's mother?" Skye asked. Laurie nodded.

Skye made a face.

They waited in uncomfortable silence. The sky was darkening over Fear Street. Huge black clouds began to roll in, angry puffs that threatened to explode into lightning any minute.

Skye began to shiver in her light T-shirt. She thrust her hands into the pockets of her jeans to warm them.

"What's taking her so long?" she complained.

"Ssshh! Listen!" Laurie said. "Don't you hear that now?" An unmistakable sound floated out on the heavy air—a child's sobbing, coming from somewhere deep inside the house.

"I hear it," Skye said grimly.

Laurie couldn't stand it anymore. She pushed open the door a bit and slid inside the Deane house, ignoring Skye's gasp behind her.

The house was as chilly as the air outside. From what Laurie could see, the downstairs was barely furnished. Only a few mismatched tables and chairs were scattered around on the uncarpeted floor of the two rooms that opened off the front hall. The stairs to the second floor were steep and also uncarpeted.

It was the coldest looking and feeling house Laurie had ever been in. And the quietest too. The crying had stopped now, and the silence was unnerving.

She sneaked past the stairs and moved down the hall toward the back of the house to catch a glimpse of the kitchen. Dirty dishes and spilled food covered the corner of the table that she was able to see. She could only imagine what the rest of the kitchen must look like. Mrs. Deane was a slob, in person and in practice.

Poor Toby! she thought.

A faint noise sounded behind her. She wheeled around and stepped back. There on the bottom step of the staircase was the little boy, barefoot and wearing wrinkled pajamas a size too large.

"Toby!" Laurie cried happily. Her bright smile faded instantly. She was shocked to see him looking so awful—much paler and maybe even a little thinner than when he had left the hospital that morning.

What had happened to him in a few short hours?

As Laurie walked over to him, Toby took a hasty step back up the stairs. He stared at her, frightened.

"Toby, it's Laurie—from the hospital," she said.

But Toby just took another step up the stairs away from her. He didn't respond and he didn't seem to recognize her.

"What's the matter, Toby? Don't you remember me?" she pleaded, holding out her hand to him.

There was a sudden noisy clatter, and Mrs. Deane came flying down the stairs. She grabbed Toby's arm and shook him roughly, yelling at him, "You—I told you to stay in your room! Get up there!"

She gave Toby a push. He slid past her, whimpering. His small legs pumped as he fled up the steep staircase and out of sight.

Laurie's jaw dropped, but she didn't get the chance to say anything.

Mrs. Deane quickly turned her anger on Laurie. "You've got a lot of nerve coming in here!" She rushed to the door and flung it wide. "Here, just take this and get out!" She thrust a dollar at Laurie who was scrambling to tear a raffle ticket from her book.

Mrs. Deane grabbed the ticket from her and shoved her out the door. With a loud bang, the door was slammed shut.

"What happened in there?" Skye asked as she and Laurie rushed down the long drive to the car where Andy and Jim were waiting. *"Tell* me!"

Laurie was almost too shaken to speak. Finally she burst out breathlessly, "I saw Toby. He looks terrible—and scared to death! Something is not right in that house. I'm sure of it. The way that woman pushes him around, and yells at him! Something is not right!"

On the ride back, Laurie sat silently, lost in troubled thought. She had gotten to see Toby again—but she was more upset than ever.

The child's fear was directed at *her*.

Why would he be so afraid of her?

And even worse—why didn't Toby remember her?

chapter
11

The following morning Laurie was hurrying past the information desk in the hospital lobby when the receptionist called out to her.

"There's a note here for you, Laurie," she said, holding out a small envelope.

"Please see me as soon as you get in," the note read. It was written on the stationery of Doris Schneider, R.N., Supervisor of Nurses at Shadyside Hospital, with a crisp signature at the bottom.

Laurie imagined the worst all the way up in the elevator to the eighth-floor office of Nurse Schneider. And she wasn't far from wrong.

Nurse Schneider welcomed her with a kindly smile, but she was all business once Laurie had taken a seat across from her.

"I'm transferring you off the Children's Floor, Laurie," the supervisor said. "You'll start this morning on eleven, in the X-ray Department. I know it's not as interesting as working on a patient floor, but—well, I've had a serious complaint about you."

Laurie opened her mouth to speak, but Nurse Schneider silenced her with a firm wave of her hand. "It seems that you haven't been helping enough, and that you've been rude. Apparently, you've been bothering the patients and spying on the nurses. You were even caught going through confidential patient records—so I've been told."

"Please let me explain," Laurie begged. "Nurse Wilton must have complained about me, but there's a reason—"

"I understand, dear," Nurse Schneider interrupted her. "I'm not saying you've done all these things. The reports on your first weeks here at Shadyside are excellent; everyone had fine things to say about you. That's why I'm transferring you, instead of asking you to leave the hospital."

She glanced down at a paper on her desk. "I'm afraid you *have* upset one of my nurses—yes, it was Nurse Wilton—and I can't permit that to continue. Edith Wilton is a superb nurse and too valuable to me to ignore her request. She wants you off her floor—and I'll have to accommodate her."

"I wasn't spying on her," Laurie protested. "Please, I love the Children's Floor! I was just worried about one of the little kids there, and I—"

"Try not to take this personally, Laurie. Our nurses are all overworked, and when they get tense they *will* snap and complain. Heaven knows, I have to listen to them all the time. You simply got in the way of one of them. I'm going to get you out of her way so that there won't be any further trouble."

There wasn't any further discussion either. As sympathetic as Nurse Schneider was, she had made up her mind to transfer Laurie—and that was the end of that.

Laurie was crushed when she left the supervisor's office. Still, it could have been worse; she could have been sent home permanently. It was small comfort, but anything was better than the humiliation of being told to leave.

Laurie spent a dreary morning on the eleventh floor, filing giant envelopes of X-rays or pulling them out of oversize drawers as doctors called for them.

The hours dragged and Laurie's gloom and despair mounted. She felt that the rest of her summer at Shadyside Hospital was going to be an endless tedium of dragging around heavy gray X-ray envelopes. *Bo-oring!* Just as Aunt Hillary had warned her.

All morning she felt defeated, but by lunchtime she had snapped out of it. She was going to try to change things—and she had a plan.

In the cafeteria she was excited as she explained to Skye what she was going to do.

"Oh, wow! You've got guts!" Skye said over the noise of the lunch crowd.

"It's the only way," Laurie said. "If I talk to Nurse Wilton, if I apologize and tell her that I was only concerned about Toby, that I'm afraid he's being mistreated by his mother, she'll listen. I know she will. She's a nurse, after all."

"She's a witch!" Skye said. "If I were you, I'd stay away from her. She doesn't like you, *period.*"

"It's not fair! Maybe I shouldn't have been looking at the patients' records, but I wasn't doing any of those other things she accused me of. I'll say that I'm sorry and ask her to give me another chance on the Children's Floor. I'll say *anything!* I can't spend the rest of the summer in X-ray. I'll turn as gray as the envelopes there."

"Why don't you wait a couple of days? Let her calm down a little. If she's angry, you're not going to get anywhere with her."

"No, I can't wait! It'll just get worse. I want to straighten this out as soon as I can. Today!" Laurie said passionately. "I'm going to see her right after work."

"Well, good luck," Skye said without much enthusiasm. "I'll wait for you on the ninth floor, so I can tell you I told you so."

Bucking the swarm of workmen leaving the Franklin Fear Wing for the day, Laurie made her way to the Nurses' Station on the Children's Floor.

Nurse Jenny Girard was at the desk, looking frazzled. She had the phone receiver balanced between her ear and shoulder as she wrote a note with one hand, flipped through files with the other, and tried to fend off a good-looking construction worker who was hanging out flirting with her.

When she hung up, she glared first at Laurie, then at the workman. He got the hint.

"Okay, babe, see you tomorrow," he said cheerfully, and left with the last of the construction crew for the service elevator.

Nurse Girard turned back to Laurie in the calm that followed the workman's departure. "Now, what do *you* want?"

"Uh, I was looking for Nurse Wilton. Have you seen her?" Laurie asked.

"She's around somewhere," the nurse answered in a tone that definitely meant, "Don't bother me." She jumped to her feet, picked a tray of medications off the utility table in the corner, and left the desk.

Laurie wasn't sure what to do next. As she stood there, shifting uncomfortably from one foot to the other, a door halfway down the hall opened. Nurse Wilton came out and strode briskly down the corridor in the opposite direction from the Nurses' Station.

Now was her chance. Laurie followed the nurse.

She was about to call out, but stopped herself.

Nurse Wilton was doing something strange. She had opened the door to the Fear Wing and was peering inside. Then, without a backward glance, she quickly stepped inside.

The door swung closed behind her.

Laurie was totally puzzled. What reason would Nurse Wilton have to go into the new wing? And what should Laurie do now?

She decided to wait until the nurse came out and then try to talk to her.

She returned to the Nurses' Station, picked up the phone, and punched in her home number. After five rings the answering machine came on. Keeping an eye on the Fear Wing door, Laurie left a message for her aunt that she'd be late for dinner.

As she was talking, she saw someone else go around the corner of the hall at the far end—someone else who stopped outside the Fear Wing and quickly slipped inside.

It was Rick Spencer, but he hadn't noticed Laurie watching him.

How weird, Laurie thought, hanging up the phone. Why would both of them go in there? Was it a planned meeting, or was Rick following the nurse?

Now what?

Laurie didn't want to take her eyes off the door,

afraid that she'd miss Nurse Wilton when she came out. If she left now, she didn't know if she'd have the nerve to try to appeal to her the next day. And the thought of spending another day shut up in the X-ray Department was too depressing to bear.

However long it took, Laurie decided to wait until she got her chance to talk to the old witch.

Ten minutes stretched into fifteen, then twenty, then twenty-five. But neither Nurse Wilton nor Rick came out of the Fear Wing.

Laurie was in agony, waiting restlessly and trying to stay out of the way as the nurses' shifts started changing.

Should she follow Rick and the nurse? She didn't want to be accused of spying, but what could those two be doing in the empty wing for so long?

Finally she couldn't stand it any longer. She made her way down the hall to the forbidden door with its yellow and black warning signs. Was anyone watching her? She didn't think so.

Cautiously, she pushed open the door and entered the darkened Franklin Fear Wing.

Everything was dead quiet inside, and there was a strange chill in the air. Even though the light was dim, Laurie sensed that she was in a huge room that was empty.

Grotesque shapes huddled on the floor—the workmen's equipment—but nothing was moving in the chaos and rubble of the new construction.

"Hello?" she called fearfully.

But no one answered.

Where could Rick and the nurse have gone? She could see no other door. Also the stairs connecting the floors hadn't been built yet.

"Is anyone here?" she asked in a voice husky with fear.

Was one of those ominous shapes on the floor something other than construction equipment? Something waiting to spring out at her?

Carefully feeling her way, she stepped around the scattered mounds on the floor and made her way to the far wall. "Nurse Wilton?" Her tremulous call was greeted with silence. "Rick?"

The room echoed, but only from the sound of her own voice—and that of her fear-filled breathing.

Her hand touched the gritty wall at the far end of the room. She jumped at the contact. Then she started moving more quickly, her hand sliding along the wall for support.

They *had* to be in there—but *where?* How big was the room?

What was that lump on the floor?

Just a tangle of wires. But it looked awful. She hated being there. She was sorry she had come.

Her thoughts were a frightened jumble as she quickened her steps. *I'm getting out of here!*

Just then her foot stepped out—*into empty air!*

She threw herself back and stood staring, horrified. There was a gaping hole in the wall. The floor, too, was sheared away—and there was nothing below it!

It took her a few seconds to realize what she was staring at. The opening would undoubtedly be the elevator shaft once the Franklin Fear Wing was completed.

But right then it was nothing but a hole in the floor, and she had almost stepped through it!

Laurie continued to back away, shocked at how close she had come to falling to her death.

Her foot touched something soft. She turned and looked down.

At her feet, reaching forward, was an outstretched hand.

Laurie jumped back, gasping in horror.

A body was lying there half-hidden in the construction mess!

It was Nurse Wilton, her mouth open, her eyes bulging.

A long surgical knife protruded from her throat.

chapter

12

Laurie clapped a hand over her mouth to stifle a scream. She continued to stare down at the body.

There was no question that the nurse was dead. The blade of the surgical knife was completely buried in her throat.

Only a few drops of red showed on her neck. The blade had sealed the wound and prevented the blood from spurting. The expression of surprise on Nurse Wilton's face would have been comical if she weren't so hideously, blankly dead.

For a few seconds Laurie stood paralyzed by terror and disgust. Then she shook herself out of it and flew into action.

Dodging the construction mess, she made her way to the door and out of the Fear Wing.

Skye was waiting for her down the hall at the Nurses' Station, talking to Nurse Jenny Girard. Frantically Laurie signaled from outside the Fear Wing door and called out, "Skye, please! Come here!"

Nurse Girard and Skye both stared at Laurie, puzzled by the urgency in her voice. Skye ran down the hall, her eyebrows raised.

Laurie grabbed her arm and pulled her against the wall.

"Nurse Wilton's in there, inside the Fear Wing, stabbed in the throat!" Laurie blurted out the news in a frantic whisper. "She's dead!"

"You're kidding!" Skye stared at her friend in shock. "What happened? Did you have a fight? I mean, you didn't—?"

"What are you thinking?" Laurie was appalled. "*I* didn't do anything! I didn't touch her! She was dead when I got there. I practically fell over her!"

"What were you doing inside the Fear Wing?" Skye asked, her eyes moving to the yellow and black signs. "Listen, are you sure about this?"

Laurie nodded.

"We'll have to get a doctor," Skye said. "And call the police, call someone—"

"Yes, yes, right away!" Laurie agreed. Her legs felt like jelly as she and Skye went back to the Nurses' Station.

"Is anything wrong?" Nurse Girard asked as

the girls ran up to the desk. "You look as if you've had a shock, Laurie. What is it?"

In one great outburst Laurie told her what she'd found.

Nurse Girard didn't believe her at first—any more than Skye had—but Laurie kept insisting. Finally she grabbed the phone and punched in a number.

"Dr. Sherman, emergency. There's been an accident on the ninth floor. In the new Fear Wing. Sounds serious."

When she hung up, she rang another number. "Security to the ninth floor, *stat!* Trouble in the Franklin Fear Wing. One of the nurses may have been assaulted."

Then she jumped up and beckoned Laurie and Skye to follow her. "I've called the resident covering the floor tonight," she told them as they took off down the hall. "And the security guards will meet us at the new wing. You're going to have to show us where you found Nurse Wilton."

Laurie led the way. In her haste, she almost crashed into a gurney with a patient under sheets being wheeled by an orderly in a surgical mask. She dodged him quickly and pushed open the door to the Fear Wing.

Dr. Sherman, the young resident, arrived two seconds later, followed instantly by two security guards in blue uniforms, their guns drawn.

There was a moment of confusion as everyone

stopped inside the door to confront the dark room.

"Don't move, anyone," the taller security guard commanded. He swept the beam from his flashlight around the rubble-strewn interior.

No one was there.

Nurse Girard quickly explained what Laurie had told her.

"Where did you find the body?" the guard asked Laurie.

She pointed to the far wall, near the hole for the elevator shaft.

Dr. Sherman ran forward and looked down at the floor, then back across the room at Laurie. Nurse Girard joined him, and the two security guards also crowded around the spot Laurie had indicated.

To Laurie's astonishment, no one was doing anything.

They weren't reacting. They weren't even examining the body.

In the silence that followed, Laurie crept up to the group surrounding Nurse Wilton.

The floor was bare.

There was no body!

chapter
13

*L*aurie was stunned. She backed up to Skye.

"She's gone!" she whispered to her friend. "The body's gone!"

"Oh, Laurie, how *could* you?" Skye whispered back through clenched teeth. "This isn't funny!"

"I wasn't joking," Laurie said desperately. "She was there, with a knife in her throat."

"You're in enough trouble already at the hospital without making up sick stories," Skye said.

"I know what I *saw!*" Laurie protested.

The tall security guard was peering down the hole of the elevator shaft. "Nothing down there," he called to his partner.

The two guards began sweeping the entire floor with their flashlights. Dr. Sherman and Nurse Girard joined in the search.

"Bodies don't just vanish," Skye said to Laurie.

"This one did. Believe me, Nurse Wilton was lying there dead not more than ten minutes ago. Someone killed her and moved her body after I left. And I know who it was!"

"Who?" Skye blurted out.

"Rick Spencer! I saw him follow Nurse Wilton in there."

"Oh, give me a break!" Skye snorted. "You're not going to tell me that Rick murdered anyone."

A thoughtful look crossed Skye's face. "Listen, maybe you *did* see something. I don't know what to believe. But I do know we're both going to be in a lot of trouble in just a few minutes. Can't you just say it was dark, and you were mistaken—?"

"What about the body?"

"Puh-lease!" Skye begged.

Nurse Girard came up to them then, her face furious. "Okay, girls. Let's have it. There's no body. What's the big idea?"

From behind the nurse's back, Dr. Sherman answered for them. "I'm afraid it's my fault—in a way. It's a running game of 'Gotcha,' and I got gotten," he said, chuckling. "That's it, isn't it, girls? Sorry *you* were pulled into it, Jenny. One of my resident buddies is into sick practical jokes. This isn't one of his best." He turned back to Laurie and Skye who were gaping at him, open-mouthed and wide eyed. "Dr. Brooks put you up to this, didn't he?"

75

"Oh, uh, yes," Skye said quickly. "Dr. Brooks, that's right."

"Skye!" Laurie hissed at her friend.

"Dr. Brooks told us what to say," Skye continued. "He said he owed you one, and you'd laugh at it."

Nurse Girard was indignant. "Well, *I'm* not laughing. You should all be ashamed of yourselves. I'm going to try to forget this ever happened."

She stomped out of the Fear Wing without another word, trailed by the security guards who were equally annoyed.

Sheepishly, Laurie and Skye followed.

Outside in the hall, Dr. Sherman caught up with the girls. "Do me a favor," he said in a conspiratorial voice. "Don't tell Dr. Brooks what happened. He's just mad because I put a cadaver in his locker. If I don't react, it'll drive him crazy. *I* won't say anything, and he'll bust a gut wanting to ask. Just pretend nothing happened, okay?"

"Fine with me," Skye said brightly. "Right, Laurie?" She jabbed an elbow into Laurie's side.

"Sure," Laurie said grimly. She watched the satisfied resident saunter away chuckling to himself. "Do you really think Girard believed us? Aren't they too old to be playing 'Gotcha'?" Laurie muttered.

"Aren't *you?*" Skye asked. "Listen, residents do this stuff all the time, really. I've got to run. I'm meeting Eric Porter at the mall. We're going to check out some new CDs and then we're going to that barbecue restaurant on Canyon Drive. Want to meet us? You look as if you could use something to eat."

Laurie felt her face go green. Eat? After what she had seen? "No—thanks, anyhow. You go ahead. I'll see you tomorrow."

"You're going to hang around and wait for Nurse Wilton, is that it?" Skye asked.

"Something like that." Laurie wasn't going to insist on her story anymore. She was depressed that not even Skye believed her. "I'm sorry I got you into this mess."

"Oh, well, what's a friend for? Let me know how you make out."

Laurie walked Skye as far as the Nurses' Station and watched her bounce into the elevator. Nurse Girard came out of the small back office, a light sweater over her arm, her bag slung over her shoulder. She scowled when she saw Laurie, but left without saying anything.

She must think I'm a jerk, Laurie thought, but she didn't know how to explain any of this. Nurse Wilton was definitely murdered, but how could her body disappear from a room with only one door?

And, hard as it was to believe, Rick Spencer *must* have done it. Killed her and, somehow, moved her body.

Worse than that, Laurie had the overwhelming fear that it had something to do with little Toby

Deane. Every time she had gotten close to the child, something awful had happened, something she couldn't understand.

Toby . . . Nurse Wilton . . . Rick Spencer. They were all connected. She didn't know what the connection was, but she was positive that all three were involved.

She knew what she had to do. Search out some answers on Fear Street, at Toby's house. And this time she'd have to go alone.

A few minutes later, as Laurie was standing at the Nurses' Station, carts of food began rattling throughout the ninth-floor corridor. Dinnertime at the hospital was always very early.

Soon the nurses were busy supervising orderlies and assisting patients who needed help. Dishes clattered, and nurses ran in and out of the rooms. No one paid any attention to Laurie as she slipped into the back office where the patient records were kept.

She decided to check Toby's records more carefully. Maybe this time, something in them would give her a clue.

Keeping her eyes and ears alert for a nurse, Laurie began to search for Toby's chart. It shouldn't be too difficult this time, because she knew exactly where it would be. She found the *D* files and dug in. *Damone . . . Darnell . . . Dayton . . . Debrett. . . .*

Where was *Deane?*

The files must be out of order, she thought. She checked through the entire *D* file, but there were no records for Toby Deane.

She was getting desperate, when it occurred to her that his chart might have been mistakenly returned to the folder of current patients.

Creeping around the tiny office, Laurie pounced on the new patient folders. Again, no luck.

Nowhere in any of the records was there any sign of Toby Deane's name. It was as if he had never been in Shadyside Hospital.

It was as if he had never existed at all!

chapter

14

"*I*t's an *excellent* car!" Skye exclaimed when Laurie met her in the hospital lobby at noon the next day.

Skye was drooling over the red Mercedes that was on display for the raffle. The dreamy expression in her eyes said that in her imagination she was already driving it, wearing the new red outfit that was a part of her bright and shiny fantasy. "I think I'll buy another few tickets, just to be sure."

"You've got enough," Laurie told her.

"That's easy for you to say. If I rolled around in a fabulous white BMW like yours, I wouldn't care about the raffle either."

Skye turned away from the Mercedes. "I don't think I can stand to look at it anymore. If anyone dares to win *my* car—"

"Come on." Laurie laughed. "I'm starved. Another few minutes on the eleventh floor and I would have started eating the X-rays."

They headed for Patsy's Pizzeria for lunch; neither of them could face the hospital cafeteria that day.

"Well, how did it go yesterday?" Skye asked over a gooey slice of pizza with everything on it. "You're still alive. Did you catch up with witch Wilton?"

"No, I didn't. Did *you* see her this morning?"

Skye shrugged. "Well, no—but that doesn't mean anything. She could have taken the day off, or maybe she's working the night shift. Don't look at me like that! Just because she's not around doesn't mean that somebody killed her."

"Forget it," Laurie said. A day off? Working the night shift? That's what she'd heard when she asked about Nurse Wilton at the Nurses' Station. One nice young nurse told her that it was really hard to keep up with schedules in the summer, because all the nurses traded with one another so that they could schedule vacations. It sounded logical, but she wasn't buying it.

She didn't see any point in trying to convince her friend. Skye obviously thought Laurie was losing it—and Laurie couldn't really blame her. *She* knew that Nurse Wilton was dead, but no one else was going to believe her, not without a body.

And what about Toby? Why had his records disappeared? Clearly someone had removed them from the files.

But why?

Too many questions, Laurie thought. She was gloomy all through lunch. But the afternoon in the X-ray Department passed more quickly as she made plans for later that day.

If she wanted answers, she'd have to head back to Fear Street—and the sooner the better.

After work Laurie drove home to change her clothes. She loved clothes almost as much as Skye did, and she always dressed with care, even though she knew she'd be spending the day hidden under a drab tan hospital tunic. Now she was dressing just as carefully—but with a special purpose.

Her dark jeans were shredding at the knees, not because it was the look, but because she wore them when she helped her aunt Hillary work in the vegetable garden. Grubbing around in the dirt and grumbling about the rabbits who got to her carrots before she did was one of Hillary's favorite weekend pastimes, and Laurie often joined her.

With the jeans she put on her long-sleeved dark blue sweatshirt. It was light enough for summer and it protected her arms from scratches.

If her aunt had seen what Laurie was wearing, she would have asked questions. So Laurie was glad that Hillary hadn't come home yet when she left in her gardening clothes. It was the perfect outfit for what she had planned.

Before she started her car, Laurie tied a dark blue silk scarf around her head to hide her honey-blond hair. She checked her reflection in the rearview mirror and thought, Just what the well-dressed cat burglar should wear. Then all whimsical thoughts vanished as she backed out of the driveway and headed for Fear Street.

The shadows were already lengthening when she reached the curve in the road opposite the Fear Street cemetery.

There was a road that cut off at the edge of the woods. Laurie stopped and parked well out of sight of Fear Street.

The heavy, dead air of Fear Street surrounded her as she stepped out of her car. It seemed to press in on all sides, and she could almost feel her ears pop.

She started to lock the car door out of habit, then stopped. She'd feel safer if she could make it back inside her car quickly—just in case.

It was getting dark. A few lights started coming on in the huge houses that rose tomblike from the deep lawns up and down the street.

She shuddered as she imagined that the lights were the eyes of some unspeakable evil searching her out. Purple shadows from the trees reached for her.

Laurie took a few steps, but her dread was so great that she was afraid to leave the safety her car represented. Then she remembered the frightened child inside one of those dark tombs.

Slowly she crept out into the road and made it up the side of the lawn to the Deane house.

Thick bushes surrounded the back of the house. Laurie moved as silently as she could and hid herself behind a large bush outside the kitchen window. A light was on inside. On tiptoe she peered inside.

Little Toby Deane was sitting at the kitchen table. His face was pale, his chin drooped down on his chest, and his eyes were closed. But he wasn't sleeping.

He was slowly shaking his head back and forth as a strange woman sitting next to him tried to talk to him.

The window was partly open, but the woman was speaking too softly for Laurie to understand. The one thing she did understand was that Toby was ready to go on a trip.

He was fully dressed, and a small suitcase waited in the doorway. There was no sign of the teddy bear that Laurie had given him.

The woman with Toby was younger than Mrs. Deane and she seemed very frustrated. It was obvious that she was having no success trying to cajole the sad, unresponsive child.

What could she be saying to him? And where was Toby going?

There was a sudden flurry in the kitchen doorway, and a strange man entered, followed by Mrs. Deane. He said something to the woman at the table, and she shook her head sadly in reply.

Laurie saw Toby's mother take his arm and lift him to his feet. Toby tried to pull away, and burst into tears as Mrs. Deane led him to the back door of the kitchen.

The man picked up the small suitcase, and he and the woman followed the two outside to a car parked in the driveway.

Laurie felt utterly helpless. Her own car was parked down the road at the edge of the woods. She'd never be able to make it there and back in time to follow Toby.

Desperately, she scrabbled in her pocket for paper, pencil, anything to write the license number of the car. But it was too dark to see now.

Forced to remain hidden, she watched as the woman settled Toby and his suitcase in the back of the car and joined the man up front. Mrs. Deane remained on the steps of the house, unmoved by Toby's tears.

The car lights came on, the doors slammed shut, and Laurie watched as the car drove away with little Toby slumped down inside.

A heavy silence followed. Laurie didn't even realize that Mrs. Deane had gone back inside the house until she saw the woman moving through the empty kitchen.

She was about to leave her hiding place and

return to her car when a sudden, terrible sound rose on the still air. Laurie was stunned when she recognized it.

A child was shrieking, sobbing hysterically— and the dreadful sound was coming from deep inside the Deane house!

chapter

15

Laurie was baffled. She slumped down in the bushes, trying to understand what had just happened. Toby had been taken from the Deane house, probably for a long time, judging by the suitcase. And it was obvious that he hadn't wanted to go.

Why had his mother sent him away—especially when he'd just gotten out of the hospital? And who were the people who'd taken him?

Fear Street was quiet again. No sound came from Toby's house. But Laurie couldn't forget the wild screaming she had just heard.

Who was the child still inside?

Was there a connection between this old house and the murder she saw at Shadyside Hospital? Or was the whole mystery a creation of her mind?

She tried to review the recent events more methodically.

The nightmare had started at the hospital, where construction was going on. On the ninth floor. The Children's Floor.

Shadyside Hospital! *Of course!* That was where she had to start from—the place where it all began.

And the person Laurie had to talk to was the one in charge—Andy's stepfather, Dr. Raymond Price. It was *his* hospital, and something terrible was happening there. *He* would care.

Laurie had known Dr. Price for years, and he had always been kind to her. Even though he could be a bit overwhelming, he was friendly and pleasant whenever he saw her. He seemed to be genuinely glad that she was going out with Andy.

She could talk to Dr. Price. He wouldn't think she was crazy or imagining things. He'd listen to her. He would help!

She crept out of the bushes, satisfied that she was about to take a very sensible step. She would call Andy as soon as she got home and ask if she could see his father. She'd think up some excuse if Andy got too curious. She didn't want to involve him any further.

When she reached the road where her car was parked, Laurie pulled the silk scarf off her head. She didn't feel quite so frightened as she had when she arrived at Fear Street. Deciding to talk to Andy's father had calmed her already.

Suddenly the back of her neck began to prickle with dread. She sensed that she was being followed.

She wheeled around to confront the menace. A car, a banged-up blue Honda with its headlights dim, was cruising slowly down the street. It was heading right at her!

Laurie dashed into the woods. Breathless, she slipped behind a tree and peered out. Had she been spotted?

No.

The car kept going past her hiding spot, slowly cruising by. It was too dark for her to see the driver. Laurie really didn't want to. She just wanted to get out of there.

She sprinted back through the woods to the road and dove inside the BMW, thanking her instinct for leaving the door unlocked. Her hand fumbled with the ignition key. She had to get away fast, before the sound of her engine alerted the other driver.

As she twisted the key, she heard the Honda growl as it stopped, ground into reverse, and turned quickly to retrace its path back toward her.

It was coming fast now, no longer cruising.

Laurie pumped the accelerator frantically, so frantically that she flooded the engine.

The Honda stopped at the side of the road near her car.

She slammed the button to lock all her doors and huddled, trembling, behind the wheel.

The driver of the Honda got out and began walking toward her. It was a man—and he looked familiar.

Desperately, Laurie tried the starter again. This time, the BMW roared to life.

She lurched out toward the road, swerving to miss the man heading for her. In a flash, she saw his T-shirt, an old black Batman shirt with the weird design that looked like an open mouth with dangling tonsils. Through a jumble of crazy, terrified thoughts, Laurie was struck with the realization: It was Rick!

He jumped back to avoid being hit, but tried to grab the handle of the car door as Laurie bounced past.

"Laurie! Stop!" Rick called to her.

She hit the accelerator hard, shot out onto the road, and took off down Fear Street in a squeal of tires.

chapter

16

*L*aurie was still breathing hard when she turned the BMW into the gravel driveway and parked in the large four-car garage in back of her house.

Her narrow escape from Rick had made her almost sick. All the way home, she had kept checking the rearview mirror to make sure that he wasn't following her. But there had been no sign of the blue Honda.

She didn't start to relax until after she had unlocked the back door and slipped inside the house.

"I'm home," she called out.

Then she realized that the house was dark, upstairs and down. Aunt Hillary hadn't come home yet.

Laurie started turning on the downstairs lights,

wishing that she could talk things over with her aunt before she did anything else. Still, she knew what she was going to do. There was no point in waiting for Hillary.

She jogged up the curving staircase to her room on the second floor, filled with new energy. It wasn't too late. Maybe she could drive over to Andy's house right then and talk to Dr. Price. Time was critical if she was going to help Toby.

Picking up her bedside phone, Laurie punched in Andy's number.

It took a while for him to answer, and he sounded excited when he did. He had just rented several horror films, and he was watching one of them.

Laurie kept trying to talk, but Andy insisted on telling her the plot—about slimy invaders from Alpha Centauri with human heads and the bodies of iguanas who could survive only by eating human—

"Andy!" Laurie pleaded. "You know I don't like that stuff. I called to ask if your father's home. I need to talk to him and I thought if he wasn't busy I could come over now. Is he there?"

"Gee, no. He's out at a fund-raising dinner. He won't be back until after midnight. What's up?" Andy asked suspiciously.

"Uh, I'm doing an independent summer work project and I, uh, need to interview your dad." Laurie wasn't about to tell Andy all the gruesome events of the past few days. She couldn't take any more teasing about her supposedly wild imagination—not from anyone, and especially not from Andy.

"Why don't you come over early tomorrow morning?" Andy asked. "You can catch him before he leaves for the hospital. You want me to leave him a note?" he offered.

"Would you? That'd be great." She started to say goodbye, but Andy stopped her.

"Say, why not drive over now, anyhow? I'll back up the movie, and you can see where a pack of these lizards catches a man and rips open his—"

"Yecchh!" Laurie gagged. "No thanks!"

"Well, how about if I come over to your place?" he asked, switching to his sexiest voice. "I can think of a couple of ways to entertain you, if you don't want to see a movie. Is your aunt home?"

"Yes," Laurie lied. "She just walked in. I'm going to have to interview her, too, for that, uh, project, so I might as well get it over with tonight. I'll see you tomorrow morning."

After she hung up, Laurie was dying for a shower. But suddenly the big house made her feel uneasy. It seemed too empty and hollow. Tiny sounds that were usually cozy and familiar began to make her skin crawl.

She felt all alone and very vulnerable. Where was Aunt Hillary? How long would it be before she got home?

Finally she couldn't stand it any longer, so she called Skye.

"What's up?" Skye wanted to know.

"Nothing much. Are you busy?"

"Actually, I was just sitting here wondering if my parents would mind if I murdered my ratty little sister. Do you know what that rotten kid did to my new leather skirt? I could kill her!" Skye moaned.

"Go ahead. Your mom and dad'll get over it after a while. Look, if you're really not busy, could I come over? Maybe stay the night?" Laurie asked.

"Hey, great!" Skye said. "I've got some new CDs and—say, is anything wrong?"

"No, I just don't feel like staying alone tonight. Aunt Hillary isn't home, and I don't know when she'll get here. She's been working really late every night, and I'm feeling a little, well, antsy, so if you're not doing anything—"

"You sure are jumpy lately," Skye said. "But, sure, come on over."

"I'll just write a note for Hillary," Laurie said. "I'll grab a toothbrush and be there in about ten minutes."

She was about to hang up when she heard a sound downstairs.

"Wait a minute, Skye. I think I hear the back door. Yes, Hillary's home. Listen, I'm going to stay, as long as she's here. Thanks, anyhow, for inviting me. We'll do it some other time."

"You invited yourself," Skye reminded her, "but anytime is fine with me. Don't forget, we're going shopping at the mall tomorrow. See you then."

Laurie breathed a great sigh of relief as she replaced the receiver.

"Aunt Hillary? I'm upstairs," she called out.

There was no answer.

"I'm up here, Hillary!" she called again.

Silence.

Panic overwhelmed her. She crept on tiptoes to her bedroom door and listened.

There was a muffled creak on the back staircase.

Then a few seconds of silence.

Then another creak.

Someone—*not Aunt Hillary*—was coming up the back stairs.

chapter
17

*L*aurie clapped an icy hand over her mouth as she listened in terror at the bedroom door.

Creak. A footstep. Silence.

She held her breath and backed away from the door.

Creak. Another footstep. Silence.

She ran to the window and peered out. All she could see was the empty driveway below. No sign of Aunt Hillary's car—or anyone else's car.

If she climbed out the window, the drop to the driveway was far enough to break her bones.

She was alone in the house, trapped in her room, with an unknown terror creeping up the stairs toward her!

Desperate, she dove for the phone at her bedside. But she was in such a panic that she knocked over the night table, sending the phone and everything else tumbling to the floor with a loud crash.

Silence . . . for a long time.

Then: *Creak.*

Another footstep on the back stairs—much closer now.

Laurie fell to her knees and grabbed for the phone, which had rolled under her bed.

Creak!

Light flashed through the window and flooded her bedroom just then. A car had turned into the driveway, its tires crunching the gravel.

Laurie heard the car door slam. Then footsteps were outside and a key was turning in the front door.

"Laurie?"

Aunt Hillary was home!

Whoever had entered the house scrambled down the stairs and fled out the back door before Laurie could even call out to her aunt.

"What a day!" Hillary Benedict said, dropping her briefcase and bag on the front hall table. Tired or not, she still looked cool and sleek and attractive.

She turned as Laurie came flying down the staircase. The calm on her face immediately gave way to an expression of alarm when she saw Laurie. "What's the matter? What *is* it? You look as if you've just seen a ghost!" she said.

Laurie found herself speechless for a moment.

"What happened?" Hillary insisted. "Wasn't that Andy Price's car I saw at the curb just now? Why was he in such a rush to leave? Laurie, honey, are you okay?"

"I am now," Laurie gasped. "Now that you're home!" She hugged her aunt, unable to say anything else.

"Tell me about it," Hillary said gently, putting her arm around Laurie and leading her into the kitchen. "Come on, I'm going to give you some orange juice and honey, to get some color back into your face. Then you can tell me what happened. Also, why are you dressed that way, in your gardening clothes? Did you just have a fight with Andy? Is that it?"

"No, no, it wasn't Andy. And that couldn't have been his car you saw. I was just talking to him on the phone." Laurie collapsed at the table in the large, cozy breakfast nook, weak with relief as Hillary poured her a glass of juice.

A sudden new thought startled her, and she sat up, tense again. Had that been *Rick* in the house? Had he followed her home from Fear Street?

"Was it a blue car you saw, a banged-up blue Honda?" she asked Hillary.

"No, it was a Volvo—like Andy's. At least that's what I thought," Hillary said, setting the glass in front of Laurie and sitting opposite her. "What's going on?"

She tucked her honey blond hair that was so

much like Laurie's behind her ears and leaned forward, waiting. She didn't believe in pushing her niece, but sometimes worry made it difficult to be patient.

Laurie finished the juice and sighed. The sugar gave her a fast zap of energy, and she was ready to tell Hillary what had happened—*everything* that had happened.

"Someone was in the house just now," she began, shivering at the memory. "Coming up the back stairs! You scared him away!"

"A burglar?" Hillary jumped up from the table. "Why didn't you say so right away? I'm calling the police!" She headed for the kitchen phone.

"No! Wait! Let me explain. Whoever it was is gone. I heard him run out the back door when you were coming in the front. Don't call the police, please!"

"Him? You saw who it was?"

"No, I was just guessing. It could have been a her," Laurie admitted.

"Stay right there." Hillary ran to the back door. Laurie heard it slam. Then her aunt returned. "Did you come in the back way?" Laurie nodded. "The door was open. Do you remember closing it? Locking it?"

"I don't remember. I was very upset. Listen, you can't call the police about this. I'm in enough trouble already."

Laurie took a deep breath. "I found a dead

body at the hospital yesterday—in the new Franklin Fear Wing. One of the nurses—she was murdered—stabbed! But when the security guards came, the body was gone—just vanished! Now they think I made it all up—that I was kidding—or I'm crazy—or something. Nobody believes me! So you can't tell the police about the burglar tonight, because they'll think I'm doing it again—making up stories. They must have heard about the body that wasn't there. But I know what I saw!"

The words tumbled out in an excited rush, leaving Laurie breathless.

Hillary sat down again, her mouth open in shock. A frown creased her forehead as she tried to understand. "A body—? Disappeared—?"

"And that's not all," Laurie said. She told her aunt about Toby Deane and the other child she had heard crying in the Deane house, and about Toby's mother, who, she was afraid, was mistreating him.

"It's all connected, I know it! The nurse and little Toby—everything! Something terrible is going on at Shadyside Hospital, and I got caught in the middle of it. Oh, Hillary, I'm so scared!"

"I don't blame you," Hillary said, her blue eyes reflecting the fear in Laurie's. She reached across the kitchen table and took Laurie's cold hand. "We'll have to do something about it. But, you know, maybe it's all too much for you, working at the hospital, being around sick people all day. Maybe the best thing would be for you to leave. You could spend the rest of the summer with your grandparents in California. I know they'd love to have you, and—"

"You don't believe me!" Laurie snatched her hand away and glared at her aunt. "You think I'm imagining things!"

"No, honey! Of course not. I've always believed you, you know that. I'm just worried and trying to think of what's best for you."

"I'll bet!" Laurie exploded. "You think I made it all up, don't you? Just like everyone else. You think that was Andy sneaking out of the house just now, right? Well, it wasn't. And everything else I told you is true, whether you believe me or not."

"I *do* believe you. I simply don't want you in any danger. You said yourself that you're scared. If you're in a bad situation that you can't fix, the only thing to do is get away from it, leave it alone."

Laurie shook her head vehemently. "But I *can* fix it. I'm going to see Dr. Price tomorrow, Andy's stepfather. He won't think I'm lying. It's his hospital, and he'll care about what's been going on. He'll help, I know it. *I'm not quitting!*"

"Okay, okay. Slow down." Hillary stopped the rush of angry words. "I've got a better idea. How about if *I* see Dr. Price and explain what's been going on? I've been doing a job for the Board of Trustees at Shadyside Hospital for the past few days, and I'm there every day."

"You are?" Laurie said, surprised. "Why didn't you tell me?"

"I didn't want to crowd you. Don't make a big deal out of it. It's nothing mysterious, just a routine audit. And I can see Ray Price anytime I want. Let me talk to him for you," Hillary pleaded.

Laurie jumped up, furious. "Oh, great! Now you're going to treat me like an idiot child. No way! I'm perfectly capable of talking to Dr. Price myself, so stay out of it. I'm sorry I told you anything!" She stormed out of the kitchen, angry and sick about everything.

On the way up the stairs, she realized that what she was most sick about was having had a fight with her aunt.

Showering the day's grime away made Laurie feel a little better. She began to plan what she'd say to Dr. Price in the morning. She'd have to tell him everything—and warn him about Rick Spencer too.

But *would* he believe her? If Skye and Aunt Hillary didn't, would anyone?

She slipped into fresh pajamas and made sure that her night table was steady again and that her phone and lamp were working.

She was glad that the only damage she had done when she toppled the table was a small nick in the frame of the old photograph of her parents that she kept at her bedside. She had been planning to get a new frame for it, anyhow.

Drowsily, she lay down in bed and picked up the photo of her parents. She studied their faces intently, as she had done so often when she was a child . . . wondering . . . imagining . . . what it would have been like if . . .

Exhaustion finally caught up with her.

She replaced the photo and turned out the light. Soon, she was breathing evenly and sound asleep.

The sudden jangling of the phone brought her completely awake again. Who in the world would be calling at that hour? She grabbed the receiver and said a sleepy "hello."

"Laurie, it's Rick Spencer. Sorry I'm calling so late. I had to talk to you. I want to know why you ran away from me on Fear Street. What did I do?"

"Are you kidding? What did you *do?*" Laurie sputtered.

Amazed at his nerve, she sat up in bed and turned on the light. For a moment she didn't know where to begin. Then she plunged ahead. "How about, for starters, stealing hospital property? I saw you the other day—I saw you steal those surgical knives from the ninth-floor

Nurses' Station. You sneaked them into your pocket when you thought no one was looking. Don't tell me you didn't."

"Of course I took them. But I didn't *sneak* them," Rick protested.

"You admit it?"

"I don't know what you're so excited about. I told you I was sent to the ninth floor on an errand. *That* was the errand. If you want his name, Dr. Cortese was the surgeon who sent me to pick up those knives for him. Remember, I *am* working on the Surgical Floor."

Laurie was momentarily surprised. "Okay, what did you do with them?"

"I gave them to Dr. Cortese, of course." He sounded exasperated. "What did you think I did with them? Operated on someone? Stabbed someone?"

Laurie gulped. How could Rick joke about *stabbing* someone? Either he was very clever, or else— Or else Laurie was very mistaken. But she *wasn't* mistaken, she was sure of it!

There was something wrong, something terribly phony about Rick. She charged ahead, challenging him to trip himself up.

"Well, then, tell me why you followed that nurse into the Franklin Fear Wing off the ninth floor yesterday. Nurse Wilton. I saw you duck inside after her. You were following her, weren't you? And you—"

She bit off the next words. She couldn't bring

herself to accuse him of the grisly murder, or to admit that the body had disappeared. Ducking the thought, she rushed on. "And you were following me tonight, on Fear Street. Why? What are you up to? What were you doing on Fear Street, anyhow?"

There was a long pause.

Then in a grim voice Rick said, "Laurie, I'm warning you. Stay away from Fear Street. You're going to get yourself in a lot of trouble."

chapter
18

Saturday morning dawned gray and chilly. Laurie opened her eyes, one at a time, and groaned.

She'd had a restless night of bad dreams and would have loved to burrow under the covers and stay there. But she knew that her meeting with Dr. Price was more important than anything else.

After dragging herself out of bed, she showered, dressed in her most attractive burgundy pants and a pink blouse, and went downstairs to polish off a plate of microwave pancakes for breakfast.

Aunt Hillary had left already, and there was no note from her. Laurie was sorry about that, but glad not to have to continue an unpleasant argument. She could solve her own problems, and that's just what she intended to do.

Her head had cleared by the time she parked her BMW next to Andy's Volvo in the Price driveway.

Dr. Price himself opened the door when she rang the bell.

"Laurie, dear, don't you look lovely! Come in, come in." As always, he looked so big and important, even when he was being friendly and super charming, that Laurie felt a little overwhelmed.

He steered her across the front hall and into his library. "Andy's still sleeping, I think, but I got the note he left me last night. Glad to do an interview for such an important member of my staff.

"Oh, don't laugh," he said as he sat her down across the desk from him. "You'd be surprised how vital you student volunteers are at the hospital. You're a great help to the medical team and you certainly make the patients feel better. I only wish we could pay you, but—" He waved his hand in a gesture of regret.

"Ah, well, you're not interested in our budget problems. Now, what's this project you wanted to interview me about?" He leaned forward, smiling as he fixed Laurie with his dark, almost black, eyes.

Laurie choked on a momentary spasm of guilt for being there under false pretenses, but she recovered at the thought of what was at stake. She took a deep breath and began. "It isn't a project. It's a problem. A bad one. And you're the only person I can come to. It's about the hospital—I mean, what's going on there. It's terrible!" She got it out quickly. "Nurse Wilton was murdered in the Fear Wing. I saw her. But somebody moved her body, and when the guards came they didn't believe me."

"What?" Dr. Price sat up in his chair, shock and horror on his face. "You saw someone *kill* a nurse?"

"No, no, I didn't see anyone kill her. I saw the body—afterward. She was lying on the floor with a knife in her throat, a surgical knife. She was dead. So I ran to get help."

"Why wasn't I told?" Dr. Price said, outraged.

"Because she wasn't there anymore. The body was gone. And they all thought I was joking. But I promise you, I'm telling the absolute truth."

"I should have been informed in any case, even if they didn't believe you. An incident like this— What did you say the nurse's name was?"

"Edith Wilton," Laurie answered, feeling a little uncomfortable using Nurse Wilton's first name. "You know her. I think I saw you talking to her at the elevator on the Medical School Floor. She works on the Children's Floor."

"The name isn't familiar, but that doesn't mean anything. I make it a point to talk to all the staff whenever I see them."

"What I'm trying to tell you is that I know she's *dead*. She wasn't at the hospital yesterday, after I found her body. But everyone thinks I'm lying."

Laurie's frustration was building again. Did *he* think she was lying too?

But Dr. Price reached for his phone. "We'll get to the bottom of this," he said firmly as he punched out a number. "I'm calling my supervisor of nurses direct. She'll know what's going on better than anyone— Oh, hello, Doris. It's Ray. . . . Just fine, thanks, and I'll be seeing you later this morning. There are some reports I want to ask you about. But I'm calling now about one of your nurses—Edith Wilton."

He raised his eyebrows at Laurie as if to confirm the name with her. "Yes, that's right— Wilton. Is she on duty this weekend? No, no particular reason. I just wanted to know, if you wouldn't mind looking her up."

He leaned back in his chair, covered the receiver, and said to Laurie, "She's checking, so you can just relax for a minute and let me— Yes, Doris. . . . Oh? Are you sure? . . . Um, yes, I do remember." He was peering suspiciously at Laurie as he spoke. "Right. No problem. Well, thanks for telling me. I'll see you later."

"She's not there, is she?" Laurie asked after Dr. Price had hung up.

He sighed. "Laurie, dear, this nurse that you say you saw, uh, dead— She went on vacation last week, starting Thursday evening. She'll be off for three weeks, and the nurse supervisor reminded me that this vacation was scheduled more than two months ago. I remember we had to arrange for some additional people to cover the shifts because so many of the nurses were going to take vacations around now. And that includes your Nurse Wilton."

Laurie's heart sank. He didn't believe her. No one did. She scrunched lower in her chair, utterly miserable. She didn't know what to say to Dr. Price, who obviously thought she was crazy.

"What's bothering you, Laurie? Is there something I can help you with? You can tell me." He was studying her with concern on his face.

"I—I— Well, it's not just Nurse Wilton." She was upset and embarrassed, but she had to tell him the rest. She had nothing to lose, she decided. "There was a little boy in the hospital—I saw him on the Children's Floor before he was discharged. I think he's being mistreated at home, by his mother. Only he's not there anymore. I went to his house and I saw him being driven away by a man and a woman—and he looked very upset and, like, he didn't want to go."

Dr. Price's eyes narrowed. Laurie could tell that he was disturbed, and probably as confused as she was.

"Let me see if I understand," he said. "You're telling me that a child has disappeared too?"

"No, not 'too'—he didn't vanish like the body.

Oh, I just don't know how to explain it. You see, the *nurse* disappeared, but the little boy was *sent* away. It sounds crazy, I know, but I can't stop worrying about—"

"Worrying," Dr. Price said, nodding. "That's what you're doing too much of, I'm afraid. Maybe I can set your mind at ease about some of this. Now, what's the name of this child? And why was he in the hospital?"

"His name's Toby Deane. He had pneumonia. He lives on Fear Street. He's only three, and he was crying the whole time he was in the hospital. I just know he's in trouble!"

"Oh, Laurie, most children cry when they're sick and away from home and frightened. But this may make you feel better. All children who live in Shadyside are automatically scheduled for a follow-up visit by the hospital doctors who treat them. They would have arranged for him to come in for a checkup fairly soon after he was discharged."

He shifted in his seat, then raised his eyes, studying her. "Toby Deane, you say? Was that his name? When I get to my office, I'll make sure that the chief pediatrician has a note in the child's records for a follow-up visit and—"

"His records are gone," Laurie said sheepishly. "I was looking for them, but they were missing."

"People *and* records—everything seems to be disappearing." A faint smile crept around the doctor's mouth as he looked at Laurie with sympathy. "I think you're the one who needs a vacation the most. What do you say?"

"You're not telling me to quit, are you?" Laurie cried. "I mean, you're not going to ask me to leave the hospital!"

"Not if you don't want to go, of course not. It's up to you. If you think that it's not too much pressure on you, I certainly want you to stay and continue helping us. You tell me how you feel."

"I love it there! And I don't need a vacation. Please let me stay! Only—"

She broke off, wondering if this was the best time to ask for a favor. Well, why not? He was the one person who could help her. "Only, they've got me stuck in the X-ray Department. Could you get me transferred back to the Children's Floor? *They* need me more than X-ray does, and I know I can do a good job there. Would you fix it with the nurse supervisor?"

Dr. Price pursed his lips. He leaned on his desk and slowly pushed himself to his feet. "Well, now, we'll see. I'll talk to Nurse Schneider when I meet with her this morning. You're not due back until Monday, is that right? Maybe I can arrange it for sometime next week. Meanwhile, you stop worrying about—well, about everything."

He came around the desk to where Laurie was sitting and put a hand on her shoulder. She looked up at him with hope.

"And, Laurie, my dear," he continued, "I

know there's an explanation for everything, and I'm going to find out what's been going on that's upset you so."

His kindly smile warmed her, and she breathed easier. "I'll certainly have someone check on that little boy right away, and then I'll see what I can do about transferring you. Does that make you feel better?"

"Much better!" Laurie jumped to her feet. At least, Dr. Price was going to do *something*. She was glad she had gone to see him.

He circled her chair and smiled at her once more. "I must rush off now, but I'm delighted we had this talk, even if it *was* confusing. We'll talk again, I promise. And don't hesitate to come see me anytime you've got a problem. You know you've always got a special welcome in this house."

There was a knock on the library door.

"Ah, I think Andy's up now. I hope I'll see you again, dear—soon. Remember, no more worrying." He strode to the door and opened it. "We're just finishing our—interview," he said to Andy as they passed each other in the doorway. "Goodbye, you two. Have a good time today."

Then he was gone, and Laurie sighed. It was a mission only half-accomplished, but it was better than nothing.

"What were you two talking about?" Andy asked, crossing the library to Laurie.

"Just the report I told you about, some interviews I'm doing for extra credit next term." Laurie felt a small prickling at the back of her neck.

Had Andy been eavesdropping on their conversation? Had he heard everything she'd said?

Andy boogied a few steps in front of her and held out his arms. "How about some extra credit with me?" He slid an arm around her waist and bent to kiss her.

"Andy, not now!" She turned her face from his and slid out of his grasp. "I'm not in the mood. Really."

"Why not?" Andy demanded. "Why are you always pushing me away lately?" He smiled his attractive crooked smile that Laurie usually found so appealing.

His charm was definitely wearing thin, Laurie thought. "I've got to be going," she said. "I'm meeting Skye at the mall. I'll see you tonight, okay?"

He jammed his hands into the pockets of his cutoffs and became sullen. "Look, if you're meeting someone, why don't you just say so? I'm entitled to the truth, Laurie. If there *is* some other guy, I'd like to know. Is it someone from school?"

"I told you, I'm meeting Skye." Laurie sighed, weary of his jealousy.

"Or maybe someone you met at the hospital?"

Andy continued. "A med student, or one of those sexy volunteers you told me about?"

That did it! Laurie thought she'd explode with anger. "When did I ever say there were—oh, never mind! I'm pretty sick of your suspicions, you know? And I'm fed up with your getting jealous and mad whenever I want to do something without you. Like, I've got a whole life and I'm not planning to live it in one place. Not yet, anyhow."

"Good for you!" Andy shot back. "I suppose you'd rather do anything else than go out with me tonight. Is that it?"

"Right now, that's exactly how I feel," Laurie replied through clenched teeth.

"So, you've got another date for tonight? Is that why you picked a fight with me—to get out of our date?"

"*I* picked a fight? Andy, at this moment, all I can think of is spending some time home alone, in peace and quiet, without you bugging me! You really don't know when to give it a rest!" She stormed out of the library, her face burning.

"Laurie!" Andy called, running after her.

"No! Just leave me alone! Permanently!" She flew down the front steps, jumped into her car, and roared off, leaving Andy standing in the doorway. It wasn't the way she would have planned to end it, but he had pushed her too far too often.

Driving to the mall to meet Skye, she began to calm down. She was sure that Andy would be calling to apologize before long, and she wanted to think of the best way to handle it. She and Andy were wrong for each other, and he ought to be able to see it.

Why couldn't people simply agree to break up without anyone getting hurt? There ought to be an easy way.

Oh, well, she'd cope with it later. She'd have a long, dateless Saturday night to figure it out.

She pulled into the parking lot at the mall and stopped in front of the bookstore. Skye was just inside the door, checking out the magazines. They waved to each other before Laurie locked her car door. She straightened up and squinted at the gray and cloudy day. Perfect. It was as gloomy as she felt.

Suddenly she saw a sight that made her heart leap.

Halfway across the parking lot, Mrs. Deane was unlocking her car door. At her side, clutching the teddy bear Laurie had given him, was Toby!

He was back! And he looked much better than when she had seen him with the strange couple at his house. Laurie was amazed and thrilled.

"Toby!" she called to him. She waved her arm in a big circle so that he could see her.

"Laurie!" he called back excitedly.

She started toward him.

He took a small step in her direction. But Mrs.

Deane grabbed his arm and jerked him back. Flinging open the car door, she practically threw him inside, then jumped in after him.

As the car sped quickly out of the parking lot, Laurie could see Toby twisting around desperately in his seat to look at her through the rear window.

chapter
19

Shopping is no fun, Laurie decided, unless you're in a really good mood. She dragged herself through the rest of the day at the mall, barely listening to Skye's chatter.

All she could hear was Toby's happy cry when he saw her in the parking lot. All she could think of was his unhappy little face through the car window as he was driven away.

She trailed Skye through what seemed like every store in the mall. Even though there were things she needed, her heart wasn't in shopping, and nothing appealed to her. Finally she just gave up and kept Skye company.

When they stopped for lunch, she told Skye that she had just had a fight with Andy. She said it casually, without going into any details.

"Gee, that's too bad," Skye said, wanting to

know more. "Is it serious?" she asked. Laurie heard just the tiniest edge of hope creep into her friend's voice. After all, if Andy were free . . .

Laurie shrugged. "I don't know. Yes. I think so. We'll see. Anyway, we broke our date for tonight—that is, *I* did. Oh, it's not so terrible. I'm actually looking forward to a peaceful evening home alone."

"Sure you are," Skye said, unconvinced. "Wait till tomorrow." Then she was off and running about her date with Jim Farrow that night and what she absolutely had to find to wear before she could even consider leaving her house.

By the end of the afternoon Skye's arms were loaded with packages, half of which would be returned the next week. The only thing Laurie had bought was a lipstick, just to stop Skye from complaining that she was a drag.

When they got out into the parking lot, the sky was dark, and the wind had blown menacing black clouds overhead. A faraway grumble of thunder filled the air.

A storm was coming. It would be a good night to be cozy at home, Laurie thought as she and Skye parted.

Hillary's car wasn't in the driveway when Laurie drove in. No lights were shining through the windows of the big house either.

As Laurie locked the door of the BMW, an angry flash of electric blue lightning cracked the distant sky. She shuddered and hurried inside.

The first thing she did was to circle the downstairs, turning on lights, one after the other, till the whole floor was ablaze. As she went, she checked all the outside doors and windows, making sure they were all securely locked.

She tested the lock on the basement door and was satisfied. Then she started upstairs.

Halfway up the curving steps, she stopped and listened. Was that a sound inside the house? Coming from the second floor?

Fear rooted her to the stairs.

Then she saw the blue light that flashed through an upstairs window and heard the sizzle of lightning outside. No, no one was in the house. She was just hearing the noise of the storm.

She hurried upstairs before she lost her nerve.

She felt better as soon as she got all the second-floor lights turned on and the windows checked. She changed into jeans, sneakers, and her big white Irish knit sweater and went downstairs to the kitchen. She wasn't going to wait for her aunt for dinner. She might have decided to work around the clock on the hospital audit.

After a bowl of hot tomato soup and a green salad, neither of which Laurie really tasted, she settled in the library to watch television.

The minutes crept by with painful slowness. She kept checking her watch, wondering how long it would be before Hillary came home. She began to feel unbearably vulnerable. She turned the volume on the TV set low and tried to listen for sounds, friendly or threatening.

Before long her thoughts started drifting to Toby. . . .

Why was he back with Mrs. Deane so soon? The suitcase he drove off with seemed to suggest that he would be gone for quite a long time. Who was the child crying in the Deane house after Toby had left? What was the connection between Toby and Nurse Wilton? And why was Mrs. Deane always so rough with him? He was such a sweet, lovable child. . . .

What can I do? Laurie thought. He's in danger —I'm sure of it. But I don't know how to help him!

Finally she couldn't stand it any longer. She had to know if he was all right. She jumped up and turned off the television set. Picking up the phone, she punched in the number of the Deane house, which she remembered from the chart.

She hadn't even thought up a good excuse for calling when she heard the phone ringing and realized she'd better come up with something fast.

The phone rang for a long time. Laurie waited nervously.

Finally a grouchy voice answered. "Yes?" It was Mrs. Deane.

"Uh, this is, uh, Laurie Masters. I—I sold you a raffle ticket the other day, but I don't remember if I gave it to you. I have an extra ticket in my book, and I wondered if it's yours?"

"Oh, for heaven's sake!" Mrs. Deane snapped with annoyance. "You're a real nuisance, aren't you? I don't care whether I've got my ticket or not, hear? And I'm very busy right now. Good-bye!"

"Wait!" Laurie pleaded. "Could I just say hello to Toby? I'm sure he'd like—"

"No, you can't!" Mrs. Deane shouted. "And I don't want you snooping around us anymore, do you understand? Just butt out! I mean that, Laurie. Stay away from us!"

Before the angry woman could hang up, Laurie heard a shrill cry in the background, a child's cry: *"Laurie! Laurie!"*

Then came the sound of a slap, a howl of pain, and the receiver came crashing down in her ear.

Toby! She hit him!

Laurie grabbed her car keys and flew out of the house.

chapter

20

On the way to Fear Street, Laurie thought frantically about what she'd do. She had to get into the Deane house and find Toby.

Was he badly hurt? Did he need a doctor?

She was shaking with rage and worry as she drove. How could that woman be so cruel to a child, to her own son? It was sick!

Laurie slowed the car when she reached the curve of Fear Street near Toby's house. She peered through the windshield at the dark houses rolling by.

A jagged bolt of lightning lit up the sky and turned her hands and arms pale blue. She recoiled as the thunder boomed in her ears, loud and close. The storm would break any minute.

Leaving the BMW unlocked at the foot of the

Deanes' driveway, she scuttled across the big lawn to the house. Another burst of lightning, and Laurie thought she saw a face in the upstairs window, but she wasn't sure.

She circled the outside of the house, looking for a way to slip inside. Maybe one of the downstairs windows was open. She tried them, one after the other, without luck.

Then she reached the kitchen window at the back of the house. *Aaahh!* A crack showed at its base.

She slid the window up noiselessly and boosted herself in through the opening. The rain was coming down as she slithered inside and dropped to the kitchen floor.

Her sneakers muffled the sound of her landing. But, as she backed away from the window in the dark, she didn't see the kitchen table, loaded with its jumble of dirty dishes.

Her hip struck the table's edge, and a bowl jumped off and crashed to the floor.

She froze and held her breath.

For a moment there wasn't another sound, except that of the storm outside. Hoping that she hadn't been heard, Laurie bent to pick up the broken pieces.

Lightning flashed again.

But this time it was *inside her head!*

And it was accompanied by a violent pain at the back of her neck! She had been struck, hard.

As she crumpled to the floor, she sensed rather

than saw a dark figure looming over her. Someone had been in the kitchen all the time, waiting
for her . . . waiting to strike. . . .

Laurie groaned and tried to get up. She pushed
herself weakly to her knees and bent over, gasping for breath. Sparks of light still flashed in front
of her eyes.

She felt someone seize her roughly under the
arms and haul her to her feet. She staggered as
strong hands dragged her across the kitchen to a
door.

Then she was propelled down a flight of bare
steps to a dark cellar. She felt her captor shove
her into a chair.

Then everything became gray and misty. . . .

When Laurie's head finally cleared, she realized that she must have blacked out for a few
minutes. She tried to move, but couldn't.

Something was cutting into her arms and legs.
She was tied tightly to the chair, thick rope
binding her arms and ankles to the chair's legs.
Then she realized that someone was leaning over
her. Laurie looked up into the angry face of Mrs.
Deane.

"Scream all you want," Mrs. Deane snarled at
her. "No one will hear you. I warned you, but you
wouldn't listen."

She gave the ropes a final tug and turned
toward the cellar steps. "You meddling fool!" she
said over her shoulder as she climbed the steps
and slammed the cellar door above.

Laurie strained at the ropes, but there wasn't an inch of give. She grunted and pulled again.

Then she heard Mrs. Deane's voice float down to the cellar from the kitchen phone upstairs.

Laurie stopped struggling and listened.

"It's that girl again—Laurie Masters," Mrs. Deane said. "She showed up here, snooping around. She broke into the house, but I've got her. . . . No, she can't get away. She's tied up in the cellar, good and tight. But you'll have to deal with her yourself. This is more than I signed on for. . . . Okay, take care of her aunt first. Then come finish off the girl. And *hurry!*"

Mrs. Deane slammed the phone down with a bang.

Aunt Hillary in danger too?

Laurie's eyes widened in horror. What did Hillary have to do with any of this? She wasn't involved.

But they were going to *kill* her! And Laurie too!

She had to warn her aunt. She had to get free if she was going to save them both!

She struggled frantically against the ropes, but they were so tight that each tug brought sharp pain to her wrists. She tried again and cried out as the rope sliced into her skin.

Helplessly, she hung her head and let the tears fall from her eyes. She heard thunder crash outside and raindrops slap the high window of the cellar.

A fresh burst of lightning and another roll of

thunder penetrated the gloom of the dark room. Laurie scanned the cellar during the flash. She saw something glinting on a long table across the cellar.

Scissors—on the worktable! If she could reach them, she could cut herself free!

She started scooting her chair toward the table. The sound of legs scraping on the cement floor echoed through the damp cellar.

She realized that any further noise would bring Mrs. Deane down to investigate. She'd have to wait until she was sure that Mrs. Deane had left the kitchen.

Straining to listen, Laurie tried to gather her strength. In her head, she counted the minutes ticking by. The waiting became intolerable. Every second brought her aunt and herself closer to death!

At last she thought it was safe. There had been no sound from upstairs for a while.

In the quiet she began edging her chair toward the worktable. Slowly, painfully, trying not to make too much noise, she worked her way across the cellar floor.

The lightning flashes guided her. The thunder helped drown out the thumping and scraping of her chair, as well as the beating of her heart, which boomed in her ears.

Bit by bit . . . inch by inch . . . bouncing the chair, sliding it, stopping to listen for danger . . .

It took forever, but at last Laurie was able to

maneuver the chair over to the worktable and turn it around so that she could reach for the scissors. Her hand crawled up to the tabletop, stretching, straining. She could feel the tips of the scissors with her fingers!

A sound from upstairs.

Laurie gasped and held her breath.

From her position beside the worktable, she could see up the dark stairs to the cellar door above.

The next flash of lightning revealed a sight that chilled her.

The doorknob was turning. The door was opening.

As the dark closed in again at the top of the stairs, she heard a creak on the steps.

They were coming to get her now.

chapter

21

*L*aurie stiffened in her chair. Where could she hide?

Nowhere!

She slumped down and closed her eyes.

Let it be over quickly, she prayed.

The footsteps creeping down toward her were light and slow, slapping each step, one by one. She didn't want to look up.

Then she heard a small voice whisper: *"Laurie?"*

She opened her eyes.

Toby Deane was standing in front of her, barefoot, in his pajamas. He was hugging his teddy bear and he looked even more terrified than Laurie.

"Oh, Toby!" Laurie cried with relief. "Are you

okay?" She could see that he wasn't hurt, only terribly frightened.

"Why you tied up?" he asked, his eyes round.

"Sssshhh," Laurie warned. "I need your help, Toby. Will you help me?"

"Yes," he said, nodding gravely.

"Do you see those scissors on the table? They're very, very sharp. But I want you to pick them up—carefully—and put them in my hand. Can you do that for me?"

"I'm careful with scissors," he said proudly.

"Good boy. Now, pick them up slowly and give them to me. And try not to make any noise."

Toby reached up to the table behind her. There was a scratching sound, then Laurie felt the cold handles of the scissors slip into her hand. Frantically, using one of the blades she began to saw at her ropes as Toby watched her.

"Where's your mother?" she asked, working the blade and trying not to cut herself.

"Don't know," Toby said.

"Is she upstairs? In her bedroom, maybe?"

"Oh, yeah," he said as if he had just understood. "In the bedroom. I was real quiet so she wouldn't hear me. She gets mad."

"I know," Laurie said, struggling with the scissors. "So she didn't hear you come downstairs?"

Toby shook his head.

"Why didn't you say hello to me when I came to your house the other day? Did I frighten you?"

Toby didn't seem to understand.

"You know," Laurie said. "When I saw you on the steps—and your mother chased you back upstairs. Why were you so afraid of me?"

Toby stared at her, puzzled.

"Don't you remember?"

He shook his head again.

"Well, then, tell me where you went that night you drove away with the man and woman in their car. Who were they? Where did they take you?"

"I didn't go no place," he said solemnly.

"But I *saw* you," Laurie said. She was breathless as she tried to cut away the ropes around her hands, but she had to find out what had happened to Toby.

"You got into the car and drove away, remember? Can't you tell me where you went? I'd really like to—*oh!*"

She gasped as she felt the blade bite into her wrist. But the pain didn't matter when she realized that the ropes had fallen limply behind her back.

Her hands were free. She had cut herself loose.

She pulled her hands into her lap and rubbed her aching wrists. Then she bent to cut the ropes around her ankles. In another minute she was free!

She rose stiffly and stretched to get her circulation going.

Toby stared up at her. "Wasn't me," he said.

"What?" Laurie said, distracted. She was trying to plan her next move.

"Wasn't me that went away," he repeated. He took her hand and tugged it urgently to get her attention.

"Who was it, then?" Laurie stared down at him, surprised.

"It was Terry. Where's Terry?" Toby asked. He began sniffling.

"Who's Terry?" Now she really was mystified.

"My brother," Toby said, his tears falling to the furry animal he was clutching. "I want Terry!"

"Ssshhh!" Laurie whispered. "Are you telling me you have a brother, a *twin* brother—and he was here with you?"

"Yes. They took him away. I want to see Terry!" His voice had risen again.

She bent to hug him, to comfort him. *Twins!* That would explain why the other child had looked somewhat different from Toby—and why he hadn't recognized her. They were identical twin brothers, and one of them was missing now. Really missing.

She had to get out of the Deane house right away. She was desperate to warn her aunt Hillary, if it wasn't already too late!

But she wasn't going to leave Toby behind. Even if it meant that she would be accused of kidnapping, she was going to take him with her.

"Listen to me, Toby," she said, rising and

taking his hand. "I'm going to help you find Terry. But we'll have to leave the house now. Do you want to come with me?"

He sniffled and nodded.

"Fine. But you mustn't make a sound. We don't want anyone to hear us. Can you be really quiet?"

He pinched his lips and squeezed her hand.

"That's right. Not a peep. Okay, let's go."

Listening for any telltale sound from upstairs, they climbed up the cellar steps and out into the kitchen. It was dark, but Laurie could see a sweater hanging over the back of one of the chairs.

She wrapped it around Toby, even though it smelled pretty ratty. She didn't want him getting sick again.

She had already decided that their best way out would be through the back door, so she crossed the kitchen and began fiddling with the door's single lock . . . slowly . . . quietly . . . turning the latch bolt until it clicked.

She pushed the door open, picked up the barefoot child, and raced out into the rain-soaked night.

chapter
___

22

Dodging around the bushes at the side of the house, Laurie carried Toby to her car and tucked him inside, buckling his safety belt.

She didn't stop to catch her breath, but dashed around the car and dove in behind the wheel. The engine roared to life.

A light came on in an upstairs window of the Deane house.

As Laurie drove away, she turned and saw an enraged Mrs. Deane leaning out, calling to them.

Lightning burst across the sky, and thunder crashed as Laurie drove away from Fear Street as fast as she could. The road was slick with rain, and she had to concentrate to peer past the slapping windshield wipers. She did check the rearview mirror often to see if Mrs. Deane was coming after them.

There was still no sign of another car when Laurie turned onto Old Mill Road.

There was a pay phone on the street corner. Laurie decided to risk it. She stopped the car and ran to the phone to call home to warn her aunt Hillary.

Standing in the rain, she listened to the endless ringing at the other end.

No answer.

Hillary must still be working late at the hospital.

Frustrated, Laurie hung up and tapped out another number. The Shadyside Hospital operator was on the line almost immediately.

"Could you please connect me with the accountant's office?" Laurie asked.

"Everyone's gone for the day," the operator said. "Who are you trying to reach?"

"Hillary Benedict," Laurie said. "She's doing independent work for the hospital, and I think she may be working late. Couldn't you just ring the—?"

The operator interrupted her. "Is this Laurie Masters?"

"Yes," Laurie said, surprised.

"I have a message for you from Ms. Benedict. She's been trying to reach you. She says that her car won't start. If you called, I was supposed to ask if you could come pick her up. She'll be waiting at the Nurses' Station on the ninth floor."

"I'm on my way," Laurie said and hung up.

There wasn't a minute to lose. She'd go straight to the hospital and find Hillary. Then together they could contact the police.

When she started up the car again, Laurie discovered that Toby had been fiddling with the radio buttons. A rap group blasted out of the speakers so loudly that she jumped. She scolded Toby gently and lowered the volume.

Driving down Old Mill Road, her thoughts racing, she was filled with dread. She *had* to get there in time! She had to find Aunt Hillary before *they* did!

The music was making her more nervous, so she reached to turn it off. Before she could touch the dial, the announcer came on with a news flash.

We interrupt this program with a special report. A car has just been found at the bottom of a deep ravine in the Fear Street Woods. The crash has claimed the life of the driver, a woman, who was the sole occupant of the vehicle. Police at the scene describe the body as badly mangled, but they have concluded that the accident must have occurred several days ago. Papers found on the body identify the woman as Edith Wilton, a nurse at Shadyside Hospital. . . .

Laurie was so stunned that she almost skidded on a turn.

So! Nurse Wilton *was* dead. But Laurie knew it was no car accident that had killed her!

As soon as she found Hillary and called the police, she would also call Dr. Price. Now he *had* to believe her. They *all* did. An autopsy would certainly reveal how the nurse had really died.

Her mind was in a whirl as she automatically checked her rearview mirror before making the next turn. A beat-up blue Honda was closing in behind her.

Rick Spencer was following her again!

How had she missed seeing him before? Had he been trailing her since she left Fear Street?

She pressed down on the gas pedal, and the BMW pulled away. Maybe, just maybe, she could lose him before she got to the hospital. Her car could outrun his, but, in this weather, it would be so dangerous. . . .

No one was behind her when she turned into the crowded hospital parking lot. She was sure she had lost Rick, and he couldn't know where she was headed—could he?

She found a parking spot at the far end of the lot and jumped out of the car. Lifting Toby in her arms, she rushed to the hospital entrance, carrying the barefoot child and his teddy bear.

Just before stepping through the door, she glanced back over her shoulder.

Rick's Honda was just pulling into the parking lot.

The hospital lobby was mobbed. Visiting hours were just ending, and people were flowing out of the elevators.

Laurie bumped her way through the crowd, Toby bouncing in her arms. She rushed to the first-floor waiting room and found a young nurse she recognized from the Children's Floor. She gave Toby one last reassuring hug and left him with the nurse.

Then she flew to the elevators, praying that one would come before Rick got there, praying that she was in time to find her aunt—*alive*.

Waiting was agony!

"Come on, elevator!" Laurie furiously jabbed at the up button. But the indicator lights showed that all the elevators were stopping at every floor on their way down from the top.

"Come on! Come on! Please—come on!"

At last an elevator arrived and the doors slid open.

Laurie was swept backward by the crush of people getting off.

I've got to get upstairs, she thought, nearly dizzy with panic. I've got to get up there.

She pushed forward against the mob and glanced behind her fearfully.

No!

Rick was entering the lobby!

He was heading right for the elevators, his eyes

straight ahead, his features set in grim determination.

No!

Desperate, she pushed her way into the elevator.

Come on, doors. Close.

Rick was only a few yards away now, making his way through the crowd.

Close, doors.

Please. What are you waiting for?

Rick was moving quickly, staring into the elevator.

Please, Laurie prayed. Please close!

She shut her eyes, willing the elevator doors to close, as Rick, breathing hard, stepped right up to the car.

chapter
23

*T*he doors slid closed.

Laurie opened her eyes in time to see the startled, disappointed look on Rick's face as the doors shut him out.

Had he seen her?

She wasn't sure.

She knew she had little time.

He'd be on the next elevator.

Laurie was so terrified, she had forgotten to push nine. Reaching out with a trembling hand, she pushed the button.

The car stopped on two. Then on three.

A few residents got on, talking about a ball game.

The car stopped on four.

I'm never going to get to nine, Laurie thought.

Never.

It seemed like hours later when the doors slid open and she stepped out of the elevator, her heart pounding, her legs trembling so badly she could barely move.

The ninth floor was quiet. The lights had been dimmed.

Laurie turned her eyes in both directions, searching for Rick.

He hadn't made it yet.

She darted to the Nurses' Station.

The only person at the desk was Nurse Girard. *No Hillary.* What now?

Laurie was uncomfortably conscious of her bedraggled appearance—her wet hair, soggy jeans, and now dirty white sweater were only a few souvenirs of her visit to Fear Street. But she had no time for explanations.

"Has anyone been asking for me?" she said breathlessly, casting a nervous eye back at the elevators.

Nurse Girard looked up in surprise at the sound of Laurie's voice.

"What are *you* doing here so late?" she asked with a flash of disapproval on her face. She hadn't forgotten their escapade in the Fear Wing. And the sight of Laurie in filthy wet clothes was not reassuring.

"I was supposed to meet my aunt here— Hillary Benedict. Have you seen her?"

"Nope," Nurse Girard said. "I've been right here for the past hour, and nobody's come around asking for you."

Had Laurie gotten the message wrong? She bit her lip, wondering what to do next.

Then the thought struck her: the hospital switchboard operator! Maybe there was another message from Hillary.

She leaned over the desk. "Could I use the phone to check? Maybe she's on another floor."

"Be my guest," Nurse Girard said. "But don't take too long." She stood up and dragged a stepladder over to a big cabinet at the side of the Nurses' Station. Wearily, she started climbing up, reaching for a large carton on the top shelf.

Laurie snatched up the phone and pushed the button for the operator.

Down the hall, an elevator door noiselessly slid open.

Rick Spencer stepped out.

Laurie gasped and hung up. She pressed herself against the wall, hoping that he hadn't seen her. Grateful for the dim light, she crept away from the Nurses' Station. She could hear Rick's footsteps coming down the hall. He *had* spotted her. He was coming after her!

"Hey, Rick! Would you give me a hand, please?" Nurse Girard called to him from the top of her ladder. "Just take this carton so I can get down without breaking my neck."

Laurie turned to look.

Rick had stopped at the Nurses' Station. He couldn't refuse to help the nurse. He stepped behind the desk, out of sight.

With a bound, Laurie took off. Running on silent sneakers, she fled down the hall, desperate for any place to hide.

Where? Where? Where?

She couldn't dash into a patient's room; it was much too late.

The emergency stairs were on the opposite side of the Nurses' Station, so she was cut off from that escape route.

Rick would be coming after her again—any minute. She *had* to get away from him. She *had* to hide. Where? *Where?*

Then, all at once she knew.

There was only one place.

DANGER! KEEP OUT!

Laurie pushed open the door and ducked inside—into the blackness of the Franklin Fear Wing.

The light was dim, the shadows long and frightening in the deserted new wing. The workmen had gone home long before, and Laurie was alone, shivering in the gloom.

Maybe he didn't see me.

Maybe he won't follow me.

Maybe I'm safe!

Squinting to adjust her eyes to the dark, she

skirted the jumble of construction equipment, thinking frantically.

There must be another way out. Rick and Nurse Wilton hadn't just disappeared into thin air.

Somehow, Rick had gotten out and then come back to carry out the body.

There's got to be another exit.

Stumbling through the construction debris, she searched desperately. Then she saw it—a faint rectangle of light in the floor across the room.

She gasped with recognition.

Of course. A trapdoor for the workmen to use going between floors.

That was how Rick had done it. He slipped out through the trapdoor, there, on the far side of the floor.

And that was how Laurie knew she'd get out too.

Right now.

It was her only chance to get away.

Carefully dodging the wires and cables, she moved forward.

There was a sudden flash of light as the hall door was opened.

Trapped.

No! Please!

Slowly, trying not to make a sound, she backed up and hugged the wall at the back of the room, her heart pounding.

THE KNIFE

A wire snagged her sleeve, and she cried out in shock. She twisted herself free, listening intently.

The trapdoor was so close. So close.

Another few steps and she could escape.

Another few steps through the darkness.

Then she heard Rick's voice: "Laurie? I know you're in here. You can't hide from me."

chapter
24

*T*ears of terror filled her eyes.

Her hand, still moving along the wall, brushed against some rough fabric.

A tall ladder leaning against the wall was covered with a heavy canvas.

Quickly, she burrowed behind the canvas and ladder.

Does he still have the knife? The one he used on Nurse Wilton?

"Come out, Laurie," Rick urged. "I just want to talk to you. Won't you let me explain?"

I've got to get away! He'll find me here!

Afraid to be trapped behind the ladder, Laurie stepped out and inched along the wall again, the blood pounding in her throat. She couldn't see Rick, but she could feel his menacing presence.

"I won't hurt you," Rick said softly.

Did he say that to Nurse Wilton too—just before he stabbed her?

Laurie's whole body trembled. She took another step, pressed up against the wall.

Suddenly, in one great burst of motion, Rick was upon her. He seized her by the shoulders and pulled her back roughly.

With her last bit of strength, she tried to scream.

But he clapped his hand over her mouth.

She felt his breath on her cheek, hot and sour.

Her only thought was, Where is the knife?

chapter

25

"You stupid kid!" Rick screamed in Laurie's ear. "You almost fell through that hole!"

Laurie moaned and tried to pull away from him. But his powerful arm was wrapped around her, and she couldn't break free.

"Quiet!" he ordered. "Just stay quiet."

He spun her around and said, "Look at that! Look where you were heading!"

Still holding her tightly, he removed his hand from her mouth and showed her the gaping opening where the elevators would be installed—and the eight-floor drop to the cement below.

"One more step, and you'd have been in outer space. Stop squirming! I won't hurt you."

"Let me go! Leave me alone!" Laurie's voice was high with terror.

She kicked out at him and struggled to pull free. She was more frightened of Rick than of the fact that she had almost crashed to her death a minute ago.

"Please, let me go!" she pleaded.

Suddenly, the hall door was opened again, letting in a long rectangle of light.

Someone else had entered the Fear Wing.

Distracted, Rick turned toward the light.

"Help!" Laurie screamed.

She twisted away from Rick and slid along the wall away from the gaping hole. Her hand touched the rough canvas on the ladder, and she cowered behind it again.

Someone, help! she prayed.

She heard a sound that was like a low growl. Peering out into the dark, she saw two dim figures close in on each other.

What's that? she wondered. What's going on? Who *is* it?

Then came the grunts of a wild struggle, followed by an explosive cry and the sound of someone hitting the floor.

Then silence, except for raspy breathing.

Laurie held her breath for what seemed like ages.

Finally, a new voice called out to her, a voice husky and tired from exertion.

"It's okay, Laurie. You can come out now."

Dr. Price! Thank heaven!

She crept out from behind the canvas. "How did you find me? How did you know where I was?" Laurie was sobbing with relief.

With a click, Dr. Price turned on the heavy flashlight he was holding and let its beam shine on her as she stood, trembling, next to the ladder.

"Come here. Quickly!" Dr. Price ordered.

Laurie brushed the tears from her eyes and started toward Dr. Price, toward the protection he offered.

One step, two steps . . . She stumbled on something soft. Regaining her balance, she glanced down and screamed in horror.

chapter
26

*R*ick was lying facedown on the floor of the Fear Wing. In the dim light, Laurie could see the bloody knife stuck in his back.

"You've killed him!" she cried. "He's dead— *you've killed Rick!*"

"What?" Dr. Price asked, sounding stunned. "I couldn't have. I didn't hit him hard. I just tapped him with my flashlight, only hard enough to stop him."

He waved the flashlight at the dark floor until the beam fell on Rick's still body.

A small, hysterical giggle burst from Laurie. Now she could see Rick clearly. The knife in his back was just a design on his T-shirt, a grisly and stupid decoration, but very colorful and realistic looking. A black handle, silver blade, and red blood bubbling down the white shirt.

Just a dumb T-shirt!

As she stared down at Rick, he groaned softly and rolled over. He coughed and grunted once, then started to sit up.

"Come here, Laurie!" Dr. Price called. "Hurry!"

Laurie stretched her hand to Dr. Price and backed away from Rick. He couldn't hurt her now. She was safe.

Rick was sitting up, dazed, holding his head and shaking it as he tried to focus his eyes.

"That's it," Dr. Price said gently. "Watch those wires. You'll be safe. Just keep coming this way."

"Laurie! *No!*" Rick shouted. "Stay away from him!"

Laurie froze at his command. She pivoted from Rick to Dr. Price, her eyes wide with confusion.

"He killed Nurse Wilton," Rick said. "He'll kill you too. Don't get any closer!" He struggled heavily to his feet.

"Now, why would I do that?" Dr. Price asked. "Why would I kill one of my own nurses?"

Rick was breathless, but he answered with sharp fury. "Because she found out what you were up to and she was blackmailing you. You think Laurie knows too. But she doesn't know a thing."

"And just what have I done?" Dr. Price asked sarcastically.

Rick turned to Laurie. "He's been running an illegal adoption business right from the hospital, kidnapping children and—"

"Ridiculous!" Dr. Price snorted.

"He and Mrs. Deane—or whatever her real name is—they've been kidnapping children from out of state and selling them, selling *babies* to the highest bidders! Nurse Wilton found out about it and she was blackmailing him. That's why he killed her," Rick explained to Laurie, studying her face, desperate for her to believe him.

"You're crazy," Dr. Price snarled. "Don't believe him, Laurie. You've known me for years. Who is this kid? If anyone's been killed, he'll answer for it. I'm going to call the police. Give me your hand."

He reached out for her.

"Don't move, Laurie!" Rick's voice was urgent. Stealthily, he edged closer to her. "I'm not a kid, Dr. Price. But my little sister is. What have you done with Beth? Where did you take her after your people kidnapped her?"

Laurie stood rooted to the floor. She looked fearfully from one to the other. *I don't know what to believe!* Dr. Price, a murderer? Rick, trying to save his sister—and *me?*

"Listen to me, Laurie," Rick pleaded. "Trust me—*please!*"

I don't know. I don't know. I don't know.

She stared at Dr. Price.

Then, without knowing why, she turned to Rick and took a hesitant step toward him.

There was a loud clatter as Dr. Price dropped his flashlight. In one great leap, he rushed at Laurie and pinned her with a choke hold from behind.

A beam of light rolled back and forth on the floor where the flashlight had fallen.

Laurie tried to scream.

"Shut up!" Dr. Price growled, and she felt the cold, hard muzzle of a gun at her temple.

Rick dropped to a half crouch and inched forward.

"You!" the doctor screamed. "Stay right where you are, or I'll shoot! Her first, then you."

He started to back away, dragging Laurie with him.

"You can't *do* this!" Rick cried hoarsely.

"No? And how do you think you're going to stop me? I've worked too hard to let you ruin everything. One more death won't matter. Or two."

As Dr. Price pulled Laurie away, Rick saw that she was in even greater danger than he had realized. Dr. Price didn't know that he was slowly backing them both toward the opening in the floor!

chapter
27

"Don't try anything—either of you!" Dr. Price cried, keeping the gun pressed into Laurie's temple as he pulled her backward. "I'm warning you!"

"You don't have to hurt Laurie," Rick said, his mind spinning as he searched for a way to reason with the frantic doctor.

If only he could distract him long enough . . . if only he could stall for enough time, just maybe, maybe . . . "Let her go, and I'll help you get away," he shouted desperately. "I swear it." He moved forward toward Laurie, reaching out for her with both hands.

Instinctively, Laurie stretched out a hand to Rick, her throat choking from the pressure and from terror.

"You must think I'm stupid," Dr. Price growled. He dragged Laurie back another step.

They were only inches from the gaping hole now.

"You're not going to help anyone. *She* is. She's going to get me out of here, and if you try to follow, you're both dead. Hear that, Laurie?"

"No!" Rick cried. *"Stop!"*

Dr. Price violently jerked Laurie back against him.

He took one more step—and pulled them both into empty space.

chapter
28

With a desperate plunge forward, Rick landed flat on his belly and slid, reaching for Laurie's outstretched arm with one hand. He hooked the other around a beam. If he didn't catch her, she'd fall to her death.

But there was no way to reach her in time.

No way. No way. No way. . . .

"AAAAAaaaaagghh . . . !"

A hideous cry rose from Dr. Price as he hurtled downward.

"Laurie—hold on!" Rick cried. He caught her—just as a sickening thud sounded on the concrete eight floors below.

Rick had grasped Laurie's hand, and she was dangling like a pendulum into the empty shaft.

Groaning from the effort, Rick tightened his grip on her wrist and tugged.

"Give me your other arm," he said.

"I can't!" she screamed.

"You've got to!" he wailed.

Slowly she did raise her other arm, and carefully Rick let go of the fallen beam and took hold of it.

Up, up he pulled her to the jagged shelf of the floor.

"Yes!"

They were both gasping for breath now, she lying facedown on the floor, he up on his knees, still gripping both of her hands.

But Laurie was safe.

He had done it. He had saved her life.

"How do you feel?" Rick asked.

"Like a million dollars," Laurie said sarcastically, staring down at the splint on her wrist.

They were sitting outside the Emergency Room, waiting for Aunt Hillary.

Toby Deane had been put to bed on the Children's Floor. The police had already questioned Laurie and Rick. So they had nothing to do now but wait.

"I guess I nearly messed up everything, didn't I?" Laurie said, leaning back exhausted against the waiting room couch.

"Nearly," Rick said with a straight face. Then a smile crossed his handsome face. "No, I'm teasing. Stop looking so glum," he said. "You were as gutsy as they come—and I know I wouldn't have found my little sister so soon without you. The police are bringing her here tomorrow. My mom is coming to Shadyside to get her. You can't believe what a nightmare this has been for all of us!"

"Why didn't you tell me that's why you were here?" Laurie asked.

Rick shrugged. "I'm sorry. I couldn't. I was afraid if anyone knew why I was here, the kidnappers might find out. If they had any warning, it could have endangered Beth. I couldn't take that chance."

"You could have trusted me," Laurie said accusingly.

His blue eyes flickered. "I didn't know that."

The events of the past week whirred through Laurie's mind. "It was all so . . . horrifying," she said, leaning close to Rick. "I saw you go in the Fear Wing. And then Nurse Wilton was dead. And . . . And . . . How did Dr. Price get her body out of the Fear Wing?"

"It was easy for him," Rick replied. "I followed him down to the eighth floor, but I lost him. He must have doubled back quickly and returned to the Fear Wing. Then he took the body out on a gurney that he had hidden in the new construction."

"I'll bet you're right," Laurie said thoughtfully.

"Sure," Rick continued. "In a hospital, no one's going to question the sight of a patient under a sheet being wheeled down the hall. And if Dr. Price was hiding behind a surgical mask, nobody would've recognized him."

Laurie gasped. *"I saw him!"* she cried. "We *all* did. I remember when I was running back to the Fear Wing with Nurse Girard and Skye, I almost crashed into a gurney with a patient on it. The orderly pushing it *was* wearing a surgical mask. We all ran right past him!"

"Yes, he was very clever, and he had a lot of nerve. Also, he was desperate," Rick said, holding on to Laurie's good hand.

"I can't believe I actually went to him for help!" Laurie shivered as she recalled her meeting with Dr. Price. "I told him everything—all my fears and suspicions. He acted so nice, and all the time he was planning to kill me!"

"You *and* your aunt," Rick said.

"But why Hillary?" she asked.

As if on cue, the door to the waiting room opened, and a frightened Hillary Benedict rushed in. Rick stood up as she ran to Laurie and embraced her.

"Oh, honey! Are you all right?" she cried. "Rick told me there was a little accident, but all the way here I kept imagining the worst, that you had—Your arm! You *are* hurt! What happened?"

Laurie hugged her aunt, smiling with relief. "Are you going to make a big fuss?"

"You bet I am! Tell me everything." She sat down on the couch.

Rick pulled up a chair, and he and Laurie explained to Hillary what had happened. She listened intently, an expression of horror growing on her face.

"I knew something was terribly wrong," Hillary said finally. "I was working on that audit for the hospital board and I found an irregularity in the books, something very strange. It was a line for expenses for a project that the board didn't know anything about—a secret project with a huge fund attached. It took a few days, but I finally followed the paper trail to Dr. Price. I never dreamed it was anything as horrible as selling babies! Or that he'd kill to protect himself!"

"You see, Laurie," Rick interrupted. "That's why Dr. Price was after your aunt. He knew it was only a matter of time before she found out the truth. He was desperate to stop her from exposing him."

Hillary shuddered. "Well, luckily he didn't get either of us. And I did find the source of that secret fund, just late this afternoon. I called the Shadyside police right away."

"The police have Mrs. Deane in custody already," Rick said. "They're rounding up the missing children, including Toby's brother."

"I can't believe Dr. Price could do something like this," Laurie said, sinking back into the couch.

"I guess the answer is just plain greed," Aunt

Hillary said. Then she abruptly stood up. "I'm going to find the doctor who fixed up your wrist. Just to know what else I need to do for it. I'll only be a minute. Then we're heading home."

Hillary leaned over and kissed Laurie on the forehead. Then she bent over Rick. "One for you too," she said, kissing him. "I'm very grateful."

Rick was only slightly embarrassed as Hillary left.

"You know, I didn't mean to frighten you the other night on Fear Street," he said. "But you were getting so involved, I was afraid you'd be in terrible danger. That's why I called you later—to warn you, to try to keep you from getting hurt. But you wouldn't listen."

"I know," she said. "But you scared me. I'm sorry."

He leaned closer. "Hey, I'll forgive you if you'll forgive me."

"I have no choice," she said, smiling. "You saved my life."

She kissed him.

"Hey, maybe you and I could go out on an actual date," he suggested, still holding her hand.

"No way," she told him.

"Huh?"

"Not unless you get rid of that T-shirt."

He grabbed the front of the shirt, his face filled with mock horror. "Get rid of my bleeding knife T-shirt? Are you crazy?"

"Get rid of it," she insisted.

"But it's so . . . so totally *cutting edge!*" he cried.

Hillary appeared at the door. "Ready to go home?" she asked Laurie.

"After that terrible joke, I certainly am!" Laurie declared, jumping to her feet.

She left Rick sputtering on the couch. "Call me later," she called back to him, then disappeared out the door.

About the Author

R. L. STINE doesn't know *where* he gets the ideas for his scary books! But he wants to assure worried readers that none of the horrors of FEAR STREET ever happened to him in real life.

Bob lives in New York City with his wife and eleven-year-old son. He is the author of nearly twenty bestselling mysteries and thrillers for Young Adult readers. He also writes funny novels, joke books, and books for younger readers.

In addition to his publishing work, he is Head Writer of the children's TV show "Eureeka's Castle," seen on Nickelodeon.

THE NIGHTMARES
NEVER END ...
WHEN YOU VISIT

THE PROM QUEEN

Every high school senior in Shadyside is looking
forward to the prom. It promises to be a night of
glamour, of romance, of ... *murder!*

Lizzy McVay is ecstatic when she is chosen as
a candidate for prom queen. But her happiness
quickly turns to terror. One by one, the five
prom queen candidates are being brutally murdered. Horrified, Lizzy McVay sees her competi-
tion literally disappear and die. And Lizzy
knows that she's next on the list. Can she
stop the murderer before her prom is over—
for good?